TAMING THE RAKE

LORDS IN LOVE #2

ERICA RIDLEY

ALSO BY ERICA RIDLEY

The *Dukes of War*:
The Viscount's Tempting Minx
The Earl's Defiant Wallflower
The Captain's Bluestocking Mistress
The Major's Faux Fiancée
The Brigadier's Runaway Bride
The Pirate's Tempting Stowaway
The Duke's Accidental Wife
A Match, Unmasked
All I Want

The *Wild Wynchesters*:
The Governess Gambit
The Duke Heist
The Perks of Loving a Wallflower
Nobody's Princess
My Rogue to Ruin

***Heist Club*:**
The Rake Mistake
The Modiste Mishap

***Rogues to Riches*:**
Lord of Chance
Lord of Pleasure
Lord of Night
Lord of Temptation

Lord of Secrets
Lord of Vice
Lord of the Masquerade

The *12 Dukes of Christmas*:
Once Upon a Duke
Kiss of a Duke
Wish Upon a Duke
Never Say Duke
Dukes, Actually
The Duke's Bride
The Duke's Embrace
The Duke's Desire
Dawn With a Duke
One Night With a Duke
Ten Days With a Duke
Forever Your Duke
Making Merry

Gothic Love Stories:
Too Wicked to Kiss
Too Sinful to Deny
Too Tempting to Resist
Too Wanton to Wed
Too Brazen to Bite

Magic & Mayhem:
Kissed by Magic
Must Love Magic
Smitten by Magic

Regency Fairy Tales

Bianca & the Huntsman

Her Princess at Midnight

Missing an Erica Ridley book?

Grab the latest edition of the free, downloadable and printable complete book list by series here:

https://ridley.vip/booklist

TAMING THE RAKE

LORDS IN LOVE #2

ACKNOWLEDGMENTS

As always, I could not have written this book without the invaluable support of many others. Huge thanks go out to Darcy Burke, Elyssa Patrick and Erica Monroe. You are the best!

I also want to thank my wonderful VIP readers, our Historical Romance Book Club on Facebook, and my fabulous early reader team. Your enthusiasm makes the romance happen.

Thank you so much!

CHAPTER 1

Marrywell, England 1812
May Day Matchmaking Festival Opening Ball

*M*iss Gladys Bell's clammy hands trembled, and her empty stomach churned. There were footmen everywhere bearing trays laden with glasses of punch and ratafia for the hundreds of guests spilling into the enormous assembly hall. An entire section of one wall was lined with refreshment tables overflowing with tiny cakes and sandwiches.

Gladys couldn't bear the thought of taking a single bite. Much less risking a glass of punch. What if a crumb clung to her upper lip or fell onto her bodice? What if one of the guests—hundreds now, but sure to top one thousand soon enough—bumped her elbow as she was taking a sip of punch, spilling rum-spiked fruit juice cascading onto her very best gown?

"Stand up straight," snapped Mother as she

fluffed Gladys's puffed sleeves with narrow, exacting fingers.

Gladys *was* standing up straight. Her knees
were locked tight, her shoulders stiff, her spine a
rod of iron. The problem wasn't her posture, but
her diminutive height. The top of Gladys's head
barely crested the svelte shoulders of her younger
sister, Katherine.

"Her sleeves are fine," said Kitty. "You're going
to tug holes in them."

A valid concern. In part due to Mother's heavy
hand when it came to addressing her eldest daughter's many flaws, but also because this was the
fourth—and final—season Gladys had worn this
white-and-pink gown.

Mother huffed in vexation, but ceased the infernal fluffing. She passed a critical eye over
Gladys. "I suppose this is the best we can hope for."

Gladys tried to smile.

"She looks prettier than I've ever seen her,"
Kitty said loyally, then grinned at Gladys. "You'll
have to try not to be compromised."

"Kitty!" Mother said in shock. "How do you
even know that word? You haven't been peeking at
your father's newspaper, have you?"

"No, Mama," Kitty replied with such absolute
innocence that Gladys could not help but narrow
her eyes. Kitty fluttered her eyelashes in response.

"You know that you girls are to stay away from
all such papers and vulgar scandal sheets," Mother
said firmly. "That's precisely how silly ideas enter a
young lady's head. Gladys obviously needn't worry
about compromise."

"Because I'm the ugly sister," Gladys murmured.

"Plain is not the same as ugly," Mother corrected her. "And no, it's because I've done everything in my power to raise you both as *good* girls. I know you've never been to any assemblies besides this one, but that's by design. The Marrywell matchmaking festival is a safe place. Rest assured that the only unwed gentlemen here are in search of a wife, not something unsavory."

"Every gentleman here?" Kitty said in wonder.

"Every single one of them," Mother said with a smile. "The gentlemen attending *this* annual festival know that even something as simple as prolonged visual contact can imply marital intent."

"No one looks at me at all," Gladys said softly.

"Then be more biddable and try harder to keep their attention. When the right man shows his interest in you, it'll be because he's ready to visit the parson. They're on the hunt for a wife. Let them catch you." Mother turned from Gladys to her Kitty, eyes melting with warmth. "Are *you* ready for tonight, love?"

At seventeen, this was Kitty's first ball. From the many admiring looks the fresh-faced beauty had attracted so far, there would be no shortage of gentlemen eager to be seen with her on the dance floor.

"I'm ready," Kitty replied with confidence.

Kitty did everything with confidence. And why wouldn't she? From the moment she was born, with her big blue eyes and flushed apple cheeks and wispy blond curls, she'd looked like an angel and charmed like the devil.

Gladys could be envious, but she couldn't carry a grudge, because Kitty was also *nice*. She could easily have been the sort of girl to hold court like a queen and demand concessions from her fawning subjects. Instead, Kitty had never once treated Gladys as though she were worth less, due to having the misfortune of being born with mousy brown hair that rarely held a curl. Nor judge Gladys for being Out for four excruciating seasons, without so much as a single flower being sent to the family parlor.

Mother turned her attention back to Gladys. "Don't forget, this isn't just your final season. This festival is your *last chance.*"

How could Gladys forget? Mother brought up the matter ten times a day, which was wholly unnecessary, because Gladys's own brain inserted primal screams of perennial wallflowerdom into every other thought.

"I know, Mother," she murmured. "I remember."

It didn't matter. Gladys's list of failings was a speech rehearsed so often, Mother couldn't staunch the flow of words now if she tried.

"You were *supposed* to make a match your first season," the lecture began.

"Mother, *shush,*" Kitty hissed. "We're in a ballroom. Anyone could hear you."

"We spent more money than we could afford to outfit you in the finest fashions," Mother continued, unabated. "We even let it be known that the one asset our family owns—your great-grandmother's gorgeous plot of land in Wales—was to be your dowry."

"I know, Mother." Gladys ducked her head. "I'm very grateful."

"You're incompetent," her mother snapped. "Your one and only job is to find a man willing to marry you. Despite four straight years attending England's one and only week-long matchmaking fair, in which every single gentleman is in want of a bride, you have thus far failed to even find someone willing to stand up with you for a single dance."

"I *know*," Gladys managed, the words strangling in her throat.

How could she possibly not know? *Gladys* was the one who had spent seven days in a row, year after year, standing against the wainscoting in the vain hope that someone, anyone, would notice her.

No matter how much her feet hurt and swelled from holding the same position for eight solid hours of the night, Gladys never took a seat with the spinsters and the chaperones, lest she be lost among them and miss her chance when it finally came.

"We cannot delay Katherine's come-out any longer," Mother continued. "Kitty *could* have come out last year, but tradition holds that the eldest daughter must marry first. It is your fault she missed a year already."

"I know," Gladys whispered desperately.

Mother could not fathomably believe Gladys was delaying a life of love and happiness on *purpose*. Gladys would do anything—anything!—to be seen, to be chosen, to be wanted. After every ball, her mind replayed each minor interaction or lack thereof, struggling to make sense of where she'd gone wrong, and how she might appear more attractive the next time.

She wasn't even choosy about potential husbands! Prince, pauper, tall, short, fat, skinny... All Gladys cared about was to find a man happy to be with *her*. Who noticed her. Who spoke to her. Who spent a moment or two in her company of his own free will.

"This is England's largest matchmaking festival," Mother continued, "and our last resort. Unlike London routs, to which we are not invited, this gathering is not limited to the aristocracy and the fashionable. Literally every unwed person in Marrywell this week has come to make a match. If you cannot scrounge up a suitor *here*…"

"Then there is no hope for me anywhere," Gladys muttered.

"Your father would have no choice but to reallocate your dowry to your sister, so that Kitty can have her best chance," Mother replied, not unkindly.

That was the worst of it. Mother wasn't trying to be cruel. She was being practical and plainspoken.

Their ancestors had once been wealthy landowners, but over successive generations the Bells had become shabby-genteel. Good blood, empty pockets. Four people on a rundown farm, far off in the country. Still tolerated at public festivals like these, yet not so fashionable themselves as to have been granted entrée to Almack's, the famous marriage mart of the beau monde in London.

Not that Gladys would have presented herself to better effect surrounded by daughters of dukes and earls and actual royalty. Mother was right. If Gladys couldn't scrounge up a suitor here in rural Hampshire, then she couldn't do it anywhere.

"For once," Mother continued, "the odds are in your favor. Every bachelor in the shire is on the hunt for a bride. Forget about the lords. At this point, even a wealthy merchant would do. Find *someone*, Gladys. Anyone. Because if you do not…"

Gladys's stomach dropped at the visible pain and sorrow in her mother's eyes.

"You'll banish me from home?" Gladys whispered in horror.

"Good gracious, darling, not *that*." Mother took Gladys's hands and squeezed them. "You may stay with us until you are old and gray, for as long as we are alive and able to offer you shelter. But remember, our cottage is entailed and will go to your uncle upon your father's death. The only reason we have the land in Wales at all, is because it was *my* dowry. We haven't enough money to build on it, but renting the land to farmers paid for the gowns you and your sister are wearing."

"What aren't you saying?" Gladys asked with trepidation.

Mother let out a breath. "I'm saying that a husband is paramount. Marriage is the only sure way to provide for your future. And mine, to be frank. If I outlive your father, I'll have nowhere to go either. Therefore, I'm hoping to come and live with *you*."

Gladys swallowed hard. As if the pressure to attract a suitor had not been intense enough already! Now the fate of her mother also rested in Gladys's clammy hands.

"If you fail to find a husband by the time the festival ends..." Mother dropped Gladys's trembling fingers and caressed Kitty's cheek. "Then we will have no choice but to give your dowry to your sister, instead. Perhaps she will have more luck."

Not *perhaps*. It was a certainty. If Kitty had a dowry, she would be betrothed by the end of tonight's first dance. Truth be told, Kitty probably didn't even *need* the dowry. By now the ballroom was twice as full as before, and almost every gentleman to walk through the door had given Kitty a second or third glance.

It was Gladys who needed extra bait to dangle. Once her dowry was gone, she would have no hope of attracting anyone at all. A life of unending loneliness would stretch before her. And her mother... Gladys could not allow either one of them to become homeless. Nothing mattered more than family.

"I understand," she said.

Mother gave her eldest daughter's sleeves one last fluff. "Then please try to look approachable."

Gladys tried not to cry. "What does that *mean?*"

Mother sighed. "It means, try to look like someone that a gentleman might want to marry, for once!"

Gladys clenched her teeth behind a painful smile and nodded tightly.

She was *always* trying to "look approachable". Had spent one-and-twenty *years* trying to look approachable. It had never worked. No one ever approached. Gladys repelled eligible bachelors as if she were covered in thorny sprigs.

"Can I try the punch?" Kitty whispered. "And each of the cakes?"

Gladys closed her eyes. Oh, to be seventeen and carefree again, when all of this was new, and seemed like the start of a fairy tale adventure.

"Of course," said Mother. "Come with me. Shall we bring something back for you, Gladys?"

She shook her head. "No, thank you. With luck, I'll be busy dancing by the time you return."

Mother didn't look as though she believed that fantasy to be any more likely than Gladys did, but she inclined her head and led Kitty off toward the refreshment stand.

Gladys assumed her usual position against the long, blank wall facing the dance floor. This was where the wallflowers stood. Within arm's reach of the action. Short a partner for one of the country dances? Grabbing an eager soul from the wainscoting was as simple as plucking a petal from a flower.

Or would be, if anyone ever bothered to do it.

The orchestra had finished setting up, and launched into a rousing reel—the first dance of the night. Couples flooded the dance floor. Even more streamed in from the nearby pleasure gardens.

These assembly rooms were across the street from Marrywell's enormous, sprawling botanical gardens. Although much smaller and less frequented, the land behind the assembly rooms boasted plenty of natural beauty of its own, with several walking paths through a pretty statue garden behind the assembly building.

Not that anyone was out there now. Easily a thousand bodies had crammed into the hall, most of which were hurrying toward the dance floor. Including… Gladys swallowed a gasp.

Her sister.

Kitty was twirling on the dance floor, punch and cakes forgotten, her arm locked with that of a handsome gentleman. Absolute delight radiated from Kitty's upturned, smiling face.

Of course. Of course Gladys had spent four long, humiliating years waiting for her first dance, and Kitty was already in the midst of hers, after being out for all of four *minutes*.

It wasn't a surprise. For her whole life, Gladys had been told her younger sister was the pretty one. The charming one. The desirable one. Though no one used those precise words, Gladys had understood the corollary to be true as well: She was

13

the ugly one. The undesirable one. The unlovable one.

Four interminable seasons in Polite Society had given no evidence to the contrary. Kitty's four minutes at a celebrated matchmaking ball only served to underscore the stark differences between their inevitable fates.

Gladys tore her gaze from her happy sister, and tried to smile at her fellow wallflowers instead.

The others were either too terrified to smile back, or as uninterested in Gladys as everyone else at the ball. After several fruitless minutes, she clenched her fingers and let out a frustrated breath. Looking approachable was absolutely impossible.

If this was how the entire week was going to go, she might as well—

Her breath caught at the sight of the handsomest man she'd ever seen and Gladys's mouth fell open. Good God, was he *real*? His radiance eclipsed the many chandeliers sparkling overhead. Gladys took an involuntary step forward, away from the infernal wall, in her eagerness for a closer look. Her heart sang.

Impeccable evening wear, trim shoulders and hips, decidedly *un*trimmed golden hair tumbling carelessly across his forehead. White, with slightly flushed cheeks. Tall, but not gangly. Fit, but not hulking. Clearly moneyed, but not vulgar. Elegant, but... *approachable*, damn it. He flashed a roguish smile that said, *I'd be delighted to show you a good time.*

His sensual brown eyes met hers and time froze to a stop. It was love at first sight. Gladys was wholly, irrevocably, smitten.

Wait—his eyes *didn't* meet hers. They skated

over the wall exactly where she stood, but neither paused nor flickered in interest... or even acknowledgment of her presence. She was as invisible to him as she was to every other unmarried bachelor.

Her spirits crumpled. Complete obliviousness to her existence was exactly the reception Gladys had always garnered, and therefore it should neither surprise nor hurt her.

Somehow, it always did anyway.

One of the other wallflowers caught Gladys staring in longing and jerked her arm back toward the wall.

"Yes, that's the finest man in England," the girl hissed. "No, he is not interested in you. Or any of *us*."

"Who is he?" Gladys whispered back, unable to tear her eyes away.

"Reuben Medford," answered one of the other wallflowers. Her eyes widened at the blank expression on Gladys's face. "You've never heard of Reuben Medford?"

Gladys didn't want to admit that the only balls she'd ever attended were here at this public festival —and that she'd never met *any* man, Mr. Medford or otherwise. "I haven't had the pleasure."

The first wallflower snorted. "Ironic. You're certain you haven't heard the gossip?"

Gladys had no one to gossip *with*. Her best and only friend was her little sister, and neither was allowed to read the newspaper or scandal sheets for fear it might give them unladylike notions. They were too poor to entertain, which meant there were no adult conversations to eavesdrop upon at home, either. She and her sister weren't even allowed to read novels, due to Mother's fear the content might corrupt their impressionable minds and somehow make them unmarriageable.

The only thing Gladys had to draw on were fairy tales. Mr. Medford certainly seemed the embodiment of Prince Charming. Gladys would give anything for a fairy godmother to place her in his arms.

"I don't gossip," was all she said aloud. "But... I don't mind if *you* do. Tell me about him. Please."

"If you want my advice? Forget you ever saw him. Reuben Medford is heir presumptive to his uncle Viscount Oldfield, and therefore far above our humble status."

"Medford is also well off in his own right," another wallflower added. "If he already possessed a title, he'd be *the* most eligible bachelor of the ton."

Gladys's eyes widened in awe. Even a man like that must resort to a country matchmaking festival to find a bride? But of course he must be here for that reason. No unmarried gentlemen attended this matchmaking festival unless they were explicitly and actively hunting for a wife.

No problem at all, Mr. Medford. Gladys would happily nominate herself for the position. The trick was figuring out how to place herself in his path. And look approachable. And be biddable. And keep his attention.

Gladys's shoulders slumped. That was too many tricks to perform at once. Especially since she'd never successfully managed any of them.

The other girl tilted her head at the dance floor. "He must be ready to take a wife at last."

"Normally, Medford doesn't attend these sorts of events, whether polite society or otherwise," explained the other wallflower. "He could have his pick of the richest, prettiest, sparkliest diamonds in England. But the truth is, Reuben Medford is primarily known for—"

"There you are!" Gladys's mother said loudly, as if finding her daughter wilting amongst a wall of wallflowers had involved keen investigative skills.

"Mother, I swear I was..." The words faded from Gladys's throat. Her mother was not alone. There was a strange man standing next to her.

A man looking at Gladys.

"Mr. Alsop," Mother said with syrupy sweetness, "it is my absolute pleasure to present my beloved daughter, Miss Bell."

"The pleasure is mine," Mr. Alsop said absently.

He was no longer looking at Gladys, but he hadn't run off screaming. The orchestra's reel had long since given way to a country-dance, which was just now coming to a close. Time stretched on uncomfortably.

Probably Gladys should say something. Anything at all. But she had never been in this position before. All her prior interactions with men had either been with relatives, paid tutors, or clergymen. Conversing with a real-life gentleman had, until this moment, still been wholly theoretical.

Mother cleared her throat with portent.

"Ah." Mr. Alsop tilted his head as though listening to the change in music. "*La Boulangere*. A new set is beginning. Dare I hope you are free to join me?"

"*Yes*," Gladys blurted out.

She lurched away from the stiff wainscoting that had been digging into her back and grabbed Mr. Alsop's arm with unbecoming eagerness before he could change his mind and rescind the offer to dance.

"Enjoy yourselves." Mother smiled at Gladys.

"I'm going to find your father. I suppose there's a card room somewhere he'll have wandered off to."

No mention of Kitty, which likely meant her dance card was already full for the rest of the evening, and she no longer required her mother's assistance.

"I'll enjoy myself," Gladys babbled. "Yes. Already enjoying. Thank you, Mother."

And thank the heavens for the matchmaking festival, which this year was apparently every bit as magical as it had been advertised to be.

She tried not to preen as he led her to the dance floor. Mr. Alsop was nothing like the gentleman Gladys had been ogling—no other man held a candle to the dashing and out-of-reach Reuben Medford—but absolutely nothing could dampen Gladys's euphoria at having finally captured a man's attention for the first time in her entire life.

A thousand witnesses were watching! Her veins buzzed with nervous excitement. She'd practiced this moment for years. She knew the steps to every possible dance, and would not embarrass herself or him.

"My dear Miss Bell," Mr. Alsop began, as they launched into the steps of the Boulangère.

My dear Miss Bell! Ha! Gladys had never been any man's dear anything before. Could there *be* a moment more splendid than this one?

"I've been looking for a property in Wales for some time," he continued. "I initially approached your father with a deuced generous offer to buy his plot of land, but he refused to sell. The land I seek, it seems, is part of your dowry."

It was the entirety of her dowry. And this was not the romantic conversation she'd been hoping to have.

"No other land will do, I'm afraid. You see my conundrum." Mr. Alsop let out an irritated sigh. "That property *will* be mine. If I must marry you to acquire it, then so be it."

Gladys nearly stumbled, but saved herself at the last second.

Mr. Alsop either didn't notice, or didn't care.

He also made no further attempt at conversation. He'd said his piece. She knew what he wanted, and now knew where she stood—which was between him and a hectare of cow pasture. Her wishes did not figure.

Or rather, her lifelong wish was for a husband, was it not? Mr. Alsop was therefore by definition a dream come true. Objectively, he wasn't ancient or hideous. He was straightforward and honest. And, to be painfully frank, he was the best—and *only*—offer she was likely to get.

Worse, Gladys could not take offense at her dowry literally functioning as designed. It was there to entice suitors. It had enticed one. If Mr. Alsop wanted the carrot on the stick, she couldn't hold its success against him.

Even if she wished he also wanted the wallflower that came with the carrot.

"I understand," she said softly.

"I hoped you would." He flashed her a distracted smile. "Don't worry. Other than eventually begetting a few sons, I shan't bother you. Between the nanny, the governess, and public schools, you won't be needed for the children, either. I can promise you'll be left fully alone."

Marvelous. Her future husband didn't want her, and her future children wouldn't need her either. Even in marriage, Gladys was facing a life of endless loneliness. This wasn't a dream come true. It was a nightmare.

"I'd like to call upon your father in the morning and make the transaction official." Mr. Alsop paused. "Do I have your permission?"

Ah. Gladys was twenty-one, which meant she had her majority. She could not be compelled to marry against her wishes. Which meant whether or not Mr. Alsop got his hands on his cherished plot of land was completely up to Gladys. She could say no, and fade against the wainscoting for the rest of her life. Or she could say yes, and at least experience a few nights with a husband, and a few moments with a baby in her arms.

There was no choice but to nod her acquiescence.

"Brilliant," said Mr. Alsop. "Then that's settled."

The *Boulangère* changed to a waltz. Gladys's breath caught. At least they would have a romantic song to remember this moment by.

Mr. Alsop escorted her off the dance floor instead.

No waltz. It was to be cakes and punch instead. Her heart sank. Ah well, at least it no longer mattered if she spilt ratafia down her bodice or developed a full moustache of cake crumbs. They could find a quiet nook and spend the second half of their set talking about the future life they intended to build together.

But Mr. Alsop didn't pause at the refreshment table as anticipated. He didn't even head in that direction.

He dropped her back with the wallflowers and strode off without another word, as though he had much better things to do than spend a single unnecessary moment in the presence of his future wife.

Gladys's shoulders slumped against the wall. If Mr. Alsop couldn't even withstand her company for the full thirty minute set, their marriage was going to be even lonelier than forewarned.

"Lucky," whispered one of the wallflowers. "I would kill for a dance."

Gladys could not answer. A sob had lodged in her throat and was threatening to spill out. She needed air. Immediately.

She pushed clear of the wall and threaded her way around the dance floor, past the gaping entrance where ever more happy festival-goers streamed through, to the half-closed garden door in the far corner.

She stepped out into the brisk night and sucked in a bracing gulp of fresh spring air. *Breathe.* She was alone in the gardens, save for a smattering of statues and the expanse of distant stars overhead.

A flash of color caught her eye, just behind a hedgerow.

What was that? A night bird? Perhaps another lonely wallflower like herself, no longer able to stand one more minute in the company of so many laughing, smiling people having the best night of their lives.

She had to leave the walking path to investigate the strange rustling, but who cared? No one was here to see her. Even if this was a wild goose chase, no one would miss her. She could use a few moments of distraction from—

Reuben Medford! It was not a bird lurking behind the hedgerow, but the handsome gentleman every woman in the ballroom had been ogling!

"Oh," she said breathlessly. "I didn't mean..."

"To keep me waiting?" he purred, giving her a slow, wicked smile so hot it melted the ribbons off Gladys's gown. "I've been dying to do this all night."

With that, he pulled her into his arms and kissed her.

CHAPTER 2

*H*er first sensation was warmth. A full-body hug of delicious, forbidden heat. His lips were hot against hers, his arms wrapped tight around her in an unmistakably possessive embrace.

Which brought Gladys to the second sensation: strength. Reuben Medford was positively made of muscle. Oh, he wasn't bulky or brawny, with limbs shaped like links of bulging sausage, but every bit of him was taut and firm and solid. She didn't feel mauled by his touch. She felt *protected*. Which was yet another sensation she wasn't certain she'd ever felt before.

No one had ever cradled her like this. As if she was delicate and precious and irreplaceable. As though touching her was a gift to be cherished, and her mouth a delectable treat to savor.

The combination was overwhelming. Not only could Gladys now perfectly understand the silly girls who swooned at the first brush of lips against theirs... but now she could not comprehend how *anyone* managed to stay upright and sensible with so many new feelings assailing them at once.

As if sensing her imbalance, Mr. Medford backed onto a wide stone bench and pulled Gladys down onto his lap, all without breaking the kiss.

How he'd managed it, she had no idea. Her befuddled brain could not process puzzles of logic at the moment. All of her thoughts were variations of *He's kissing me!* and *He's still kissing me!* and *I like this!* followed quickly by *I like him!* and *He likes me, too!*

She could scarcely fathom that he'd secretly been watching her, just as she'd been watching him.

"I've been dying to do this all night" were his exact words. Dying to wrap his arms around Gladys and kiss her senseless! Him! Her!

Obviously she was going to have to politely decline Mr. Alsop's begrudging proposal. He was more likely to kiss the hallowed dirt in Wales than show Gladys even a fraction of Mr. Medford's passion. Now that she knew what a husband's embrace could be like, she could not bear the thought of subjecting herself to six decades of loneliness and isolation.

Not when she could be in a marriage like... *this.*

Giddiness overtook her, as though she'd drunk far too much ratafia, despite not having imbibed a single drop. There was no trace of alcohol in her system. It was Mr. Medford who made her feel drunk, each kiss more intoxicating than the last.

She hoped he would never stop, and didn't know how to say so—or even if she should. She might have practiced every step of every dance in hopes of one day being invited onto the floor, but she didn't have the least notion what to do in a situation like this. All she could do was grip his arms and hold on tight as he kissed her.

Phase one: look approachable. Accomplished. Full marks. She'd looked *so* approachable, he'd literally plucked her up off the grass and into his waiting arms. When it came to Mr. Medford, Gladys was the supreme empress of looking approachable. Huggable. Kissable. Irresistible.

So… what followed? She had never achieved phase one before, and had no idea what steps to take next. Kiss him back was the obvious answer, which she was doing with every fiber of her being.

She had no experience in these matters, which meant she was essentially copying his moves, pressing harder when he did, softer when he relaxed. Parting her lips when he did, opening her mouth like he did, losing her bloody mind when the tip of his tongue brushed hers and electrified every nerve ending throughout her body.

She was almost certain Mr. Alsop had no idea how to kiss like this, and even if he thought he did, he would be nowhere near as competent in the matter as Mr. Medford. Gladys was practically a puddle in this gentleman's arms, and he still found ways to stoke the heat even higher. Even her nipples were reacting to the kiss, pushing out through the fabric of her bodice as though they too wished to rub themselves against Mr. Medford's sensual tongue.

He hadn't paused once. Hadn't checked his pocket watch, glanced over her shoulder, or tapped his foot with impatience. She wasn't boring him unconscious. By all appearances, there was nowhere Mr. Medford would rather be, and nothing Mr. Medford would rather do, than sit here on this hard stone bench in the middle of a chilly night with tiny, mousy Gladys Bell perched on his lap.

Panic crept beneath the pleasure of his kisses. Mr. Medford had given her more attention in the past ten minutes than her one-and-only suitor intended to show her in their entire shared lifetimes. She couldn't lose it. Not this passion, not these kisses, and certainly not Mr. Medford.

He was supposed to be untouchable—yet here he was, touching her. Gladys was doing what every other wallflower had only dreamed of. What *she* had only dreamed of. Now, how could she keep the dream from ending?

One kiss wasn't enough. According to Mother, this meant Mr. Medford had selected her to be his bride. Even the wallflowers had said he was on the hunt for a wife. Why he'd set his sights on Gladys, she could not fathom, but she was determined not to lose his attention now that she had it.

Not because Mr. Medford was handsome or wealthy or a potential future viscount, but because he *saw* her. Because he *picked* her. Because he wanted her and found her desirable.

All of which required immediate action.

If Gladys didn't secure an official marriage proposal, here and now, in the morning it would be too late. Mr. Alsop would show up at the hotel willing to saddle himself with Gladys if it meant getting his hands on the pasture in Wales, and Gladys's father would sign the betrothal contract without blinking an eye.

The first banns would be read tomorrow afternoon, and the unhappy marriage would take place a fortnight hence... unless Mr. Alsop was so eager to gain possession of the promised land that he procured a special license and married Gladys within days.

Whichever suitor was first to present himself to her father would be the one Gladys ended up married to. It *couldn't* be Mr. Alsop. Not now and not ever. She wanted *this*. She needed Reuben Medford. But how could she convince the man every unmarried young lady lusted for to choose *her*?

Wait! A wave of relieved laughter bubbled up inside her and she had to tamp it down. For goodness sake, Gladys was tying herself into knots over nothing! She wouldn't have to convince Mr. Medford to make an explicit offer for her. This *was* his offer.

After all, this was a *matchmaking* ball at a *matchmaking* festival. Mother had explained dozens of times that the only rakes present were of the reformed variety. Every unwed gentleman in this assembly room was not only perfectly marriageable but actively on the hunt for a bride—Mr. Medford included. He'd said out loud and to her face that he'd been dying to make her his all night. What clearer sign did Gladys need that Mr. Medford had chosen her as his bride?

Gladys couldn't begin to guess what had made her stand out from all the rest, but she supposed that was the power of love at first sight. Logic didn't enter into the matter. When in the presence of one's true match, the heart knew what it wanted.

"I could lose myself in your kisses forever, Lady Midnight," Mr. Medford murmured against Gladys's lips.

Doubt crept along her skin. She pulled away from his kiss. "I'm Gladys Bell, not Lady Midnight."

He cradled her face and kissed her again. "Mm, yes, I know. Obviously Lady Midnight isn't your real name. It's a private jest between lovers, isn't it? At least, it will be, once I get you out of this gown…"

He knew her name. Her head swam with relief and euphoria. He hadn't confused her with someone else. Lady Midnight was only a nickname. He was aware she was Gladys Bell, and the knowledge didn't repulse him. The opposite! He wanted to make *love* to her. No one had ever wanted to make love to her before! This boded very well for a happy marriage. No reluctant begetting of heirs, here. Mr. Medford would visit her bedchamber frequently and lustily.

If part of his love play involved a silly pet name, well… Who was Gladys to complain? She'd actually never had a pet name before. Well, other than her sister calling her "Gladdie the Laddie" the time a nine-year-old Gladys had strutted around in their father's supper coat, its black tails dragging along the parquet behind her. "Lady Midnight" was ever so much nicer than *that.*

"How about a special midnight kiss?" Mr. Medford murmured against Gladys's throat.

"You've been kissing me," she said in confusion.

He lifted his eyes to hers. "I'll never have enough of your kisses."

"Then kiss me again, Lord Midnight," she said boldly and breathlessly.

"That's Lord of the Stars to you," he teased, then claimed her mouth anew. "I've been eager for you all night. I feel as though I've been waiting for you all of my life."

Well, if that wasn't the most romantic proposal Gladys had ever heard! "Well, now that you've found me, we can spend the rest of our—"

Mr. Medford's kiss swallowed up the last of her coherent thoughts.

By the time her brain managed to string a few syllables together, their frantic embraces had become delightfully—if worryingly—torrid. Gladys's painstakingly curled hair was now hopelessly disheveled. Mr. Medford's hand was now... Good God... on her *breast*?

There was no hiding the state of her nipples from him now. They were poking out in the night air, taking turns being toyed with between his fingers.

The sensation awakened all sorts of things she was pretty certain ought to stay dormant at a public venue, which was neither the time nor the place to act on this avalanche of new feelings.

Mr. Medford could not possibly intend to consummate their betrothal out here in the garden... Could he? In any case, Gladys could not possibly do so, not until the betrothal contract was signed.

Then again, she supposed that by ton standards, she was already well and compromised. Had been so, in fact, ever since they shared their first kiss. Progressing from kissing to touching guaranteed a wedding was imminent. Perhaps Mr. Medford was the one with a special license in his pocket, just waiting for the first chance to tug Gladys down the aisle.

Her unfathomable success tonight made her head spin. She'd known the week-long fête was a matchmaking festival, and she'd heard that every bachelor present was on the hunt for a bride, but she hadn't understood what those circumstances meant for *her* until tonight. She'd barely been here an hour, and had experienced one first after another. Her first dance, her first proposal, her first kiss, her *second* suitor…

If this were London, she might have feared she'd found herself in the arms of a rake. But no rakehell, London-bred or otherwise, would have picked Gladys above all the rest or even recognized her name. Mr. Medford didn't only know exactly who she was, he had been seeking her all along. His kisses were nothing short of transcendent. It wouldn't feel this good if it weren't true love on both sides.

His accelerated time frame might not be the traditional courtship Gladys had always dreamt of, but it was certainly expedient. Why drag out the suspense for the entire week of the festival, if they were ready to pick permanent partners here and now?

"Lady Midnight…" His kisses trailed down her neck toward her exposed bosom. "Why don't you wrap those gorgeous legs about my hips whilst I—"

"*Gladys!*" called a voice from the other side of the garden. Kitty's voice. Yelling for her sister from the open doorway of the ballroom. "Gladys, are you out here?"

Oh, she was definitely out here.

"*Gladys?*" Mother's voice joined Kitty's. "Gladys Maria Bell!"

Her parents were going to be thrilled to learn their eldest daughter's future husband was in line to a title. Gladys's sister would positively *goggle* to discover Gladdie the Laddie had hooked the finest catch in all of England.

But not like this.

She pushed Mr. Medford away and tucked her bosom back into her bodice. "I must go."

"Go where?" He tried to kiss her again. "Why?"

She wiggled out of his embrace. "They're calling me. I'll see you in the morning."

He blinked at her. "What?"

"The Blushing Maid Inn, on the main street. Second floor, left hand side, suite twelve. Arrive before ten or Mr. Alsop will beat you there and we'll lose our chance."

"Ten o'clock... *a.m.?*" Mr. Medford recoiled in comical horror. "That's the crack of dawn!"

"Then call me Lady Dawn." Gladys gave him a peck on the cheek. She couldn't wait to see her parents' reaction to a marriage proposal from the heir to a viscountcy. "You must know that my answer is an enthusiastic yes. Don't be late. I'll be holding my breath."

He reached for her. "Yes, of course I'll come to your hotel, but first—"

Of course, he said. Of course he would offer for her first thing in the morning. Could anything be more splendid? Another kiss or three, perhaps. And whatever came after. Gladys danced out of range before temptation could melt her back into his arms. They would have the rest of their lives to succumb to passion. They could survive a few scant hours apart.

Gladys raced around the hedgerow and over the grass and back up the walking path toward the open ballroom door.

As she burst back into the main room, she nearly toppled over her very shocked sister.

"Dear God," said Kitty. "What happened to your hair? Are those bits of *leaves* stuck in it?"

Gladys batted absently at her ruined coiffure as she glanced over Kitty's shoulders. "Where's Mother?"

Kitty pointed. "She went to look for you by the refreshment table."

Gladys looped her arm with her sister and dragged her toward the punch and cakes. "I have the very best news. You are never going to *believe* who fell for me. I'm going to be a bride!"

CHAPTER 3

$\mathcal{I}$n utter confusion, Reuben stared at the empty space on his lap where Lady Midnight had been just moments ago.

Women did not run from him. Women ran *to* him. They threw themselves at his feet, in his arms, on his cock. He had to bat them away like horseflies. Lady Midnight's impromptu flight from his embrace made absolutely no sense whatsoever.

Meeting here had been *her* idea.

Reuben hadn't wanted to come within a hundred miles of the Marrywell Festival of Abject Desperation. Would not have done so, in fact, had Viscount Oldfield not ordered him to do so. Oldfield was his paternal uncle, which was the only paternal thing about him. Reuben had spent a fruitless childhood trying to earn his only remaining family member's affection, only to be told he wasn't worth anyone's time. The viscount wouldn't even bother ordering Reuben about, if it weren't for the pesky rules of primogeniture forcing a connection.

Reuben had ceased being under the viscount's thumb five years ago, when Reuben had come into his majority and an inheritance. He *could* have ignored his uncle's latest summons to join him at the festival. But the viscount was the only relative Reuben had left.

His uncle also possessed an aging cat that Reuben had missed dearly ever since moving out on his own. It would not be an exaggeration to say that the real reason Reuben was in Marrywell was to chase after a graying puss called Lucifur.

Not that Lucifur appreciated Reuben's presence. Nor did anyone else, not really. It wasn't just that he wasn't the marrying type… he wasn't marriageable. No one wanted to be his bride, and with good reason. He wasn't worth much in that regard. But he had learned to be tolerable in small doses.

Take Lady Midnight, for example. She had been *eager* for Reuben's company. Persistent. The delectable Lady Midnight had sent three letters a day until he'd agreed to meet.

She had picked the time, she'd picked the place, and she'd picked the activity: two naked, sweaty bodies coupling beneath the stars. She'd been after him for *weeks* to agree to this assignation. And then, when the good part was just getting started…

There had been a brief moment when he might have been able to dash and stop her before she reentered the ballroom. Reuben hadn't moved from the bench in time—or at all—because the thought didn't even occur to him until after she'd disappeared.

He had never once been in a position that required chasing after a woman. The opposite. In six-and-twenty years of being the ton's most storied rakehell, no woman had ever voluntarily quit his side. Which was the primary reason he met Lady Midnight out here in a public garden, rather than invite her to Reuben's private quarters at the inn.

Kicking a woman out of one's rooms was distasteful to all parties. *Much* easier for him to be the one to leave.

Usually, he prided himself on never indulging more than a single dalliance with any lover, then quickly forgetting her and moving on. Yet in this case, his planned tryst with Lady Midnight had not only left Reuben uncomfortably aroused, but also phenomenally, incomprehensibly, unsatisfied.

He had been *so close* to tasting her breasts. To nuzzling between them, to lifting her skirts and burying himself between her thighs.

Lady Midnight had become a mystery.

Reuben hated mysteries.

This was why he preferred histories to novels. Things that were concrete, and true, and *over*. No mucking about wondering what to do or say, or why this instead of that. All the answers were right there, in page after page of stark facts, just as Reuben liked it.

When lured from his library to trysts like this one, he was a man of equally straightforward desires: to couple with as many women as possible. *Eligible* women, that was. By which he meant *in*eligible. Reuben stayed far away from virgins and debutantes. Lonely widow? Come hither. Unhappily married? No scruples here. Independent woman enjoying the freedoms of spinsterhood? She was free to ride his cock all night long.

Lady Midnight's anonymous letters had left no doubt that she was exactly Reuben's type: sensual, experienced, explicit. She knew what she wanted, and she'd spelt out each deliciously carnal act with mouthwatering precision.

So… why the devil had she left? In hindsight, he supposed she'd been acting oddly from the first. Like a shy ingenue, rather than a randy widow.

Reuben didn't mind a bit of make-believe. He'd spent plenty of nights with actresses, several of which stayed in character as their starring roles—or something significantly naughtier. "Oh no, don't despoil me, you wicked highwayman; I'm an innocent virgin!" was a popular game.

Not the script he'd been expecting tonight, but then again, nothing about his encounter with Lady Midnight had gone as expected.

With a sigh, Reuben rose to his feet and brushed the wrinkles from his evening attire. The night was young. There was plenty of time to go back to the inn and try to coax a purr out of Lucifur, or perhaps resume reading his latest tome on ancient Egypt's several known female rulers.

Better yet, mayhap Reuben could find Lady Midnight and drag her back out here to the garden to indulge their shared desires.

Problem was, he hadn't got a good look at her. The stars were out, but the moon was not. Just enough light to indicate he might have recognized her if he knew her well, but not enough light for a detailed view of her features. To his consternation, despite giving her body his full attention whilst she sat on his lap, Reuben would not be able to pick her out of a crowd.

As for giving anything she'd *said* any of his attention… Damn it! These encounters were never political arguments or philosophical debates. It was just *kiss me here* and *touch me there*, if there were any words at all.

With frustration, he recalled that she might have said her real name. "I'm not Lady Midnight,

I'm..." Nothing. Whatever name she'd said had disappeared into the night like a puff of air. He hadn't paid attention, because it hadn't mattered. They had met for one reason only, and were meant to consummate that reason, after which he would move on to the next woman.

Except the only woman he could think about was—

"Lord of the Stars?" purred a familiar voice. "Are you still out here?"

Reuben sprinted out from behind the hedgerow fast enough to ignite sparks on the soles of his boots. He came to an immediate and sudden stop.

There, on the walking path before him, was a sultry-looking woman a decade older than him. This was not his Lady Midnight. This was the wife of an elderly earl in the House of Lords.

"You waited!" She ran up to Reuben and threw her perfumed arms about his neck. "It's me, Lady Midnight. It took forever to get away from... oh, that's not important. I'm here now. I trust my letters left no doubt as to what I want?"

Bloody hell.

Reuben swung her behind the hedgerow and out of sight from the barely-ajar ballroom door, the muscles of his limbs reacting with pure instinct. He'd done this dance countless times, and was appalled to realize he was no longer interested in fulfilling the promised fantasies. At least, not with the woman currently in his arms.

If this was Lady Midnight... then who the devil was the woman Reuben had been making love to? The baffling, ephemeral Lady Crack of Dawn?

It was difficult to think it through, what with the real Lady Midnight pawing at him and gnawing at his mouth. Reuben supposed this was his cue to retake his seat on the stone bench, but he couldn't quite force himself to tup this woman in the same spot he'd intended to make love to Lady Dawn.

He'd never taken himself for a romantic fool. Indeed, he'd laugh in the face of anyone who suggested such nonsense. Nonetheless, Reuben carried Lady Midnight deeper into the garden until he found a further, colder stone bench that didn't remind him of Lady Dawn.

At least, it wasn't *supposed* to remind him of Lady Dawn. During most sexual rendezvous, Reuben had no trouble losing himself in the moment. Unfortunately, he hadn't stopped thinking of Lady Dawn since the moment she left. Couldn't stop thinking of her even now, wishing it were *her* mouth devouring his, *her* naked breasts in his hands, *her* legs wrapped about him.

He was going to do whatever it took to find the mysterious Lady Dawn. Her name would be the next conquest on his list if it were the last thing Reuben accomplished.

"Ohh," moaned Lady Midnight. "*Oh!*"

He lifted her off his hips without reaching climax himself. Now that he'd fulfilled his promise to pleasure Lady Midnight, Reuben had no interest in tarrying with her any longer. Not when there was a vixen out there called Lady Dawn to find and to tup. She'd invited him to do just that tomorrow morning at the Blushing Maid Inn, but he had no intention of waiting that long. If she was still here in the ballroom...

He adjusted his breeches and straightened his cravat. "You were lovely, darling, but I fear I must go."

Lady Midnight, well-practiced in these sorts of

trysts, didn't want a prolonged goodbye any more than Reuben did. She was already straightening her gown, and paused only to blow him a coquettish kiss. "You know how to reach me when you want to do it again."

He flashed a distracted smile and hurried into the building.

Assembly rooms were battlefields Reuben normally attempted to avoid. Too full of the nubile marriageable types he did his best to stay far away from. For their sake, not Reuben's. As his uncle always said, Reuben was a good-for-nothing wastrel who would never amount to anything. Eligible women were only interested in him because he was heir presumptive to the viscountcy.

Not that *that* would last for long, either. Oldfield was here to find a bride. As soon as there were two or three tots in direct line to the title, Reuben would have nothing at all to offer a lady of quality.

His rakish exterior was nothing more than decorative candles and cut flowers. No matter how pretty they were today, they'd be wilted and falling apart within a week. He was flash and smoke, with no substance. A firework on a dark night. Thrilling to interact with for a brief moment, but not something you'd want to clutch in your hands or hug tight.

Reuben would know. Everyone he'd ever loved had left him or died. He was determined not to make ties or allow anyone close enough to hurt him. Again. Even his one-time guardian and last remaining uncle could not be bothered to pretend affection. Lucifur's tail wrapping around Reuben's ankle was the closest he ever came to receiving a friendly embrace.

That was why it was so much safer to stay in the box he'd created for himself. He was a lump of sugar in a cup of tea. He brought pleasure in the moment and then disappeared forever. And even then, he was only palatable while the cup was still hot. If tea sat there in front of you for too long, it lost its appeal and you'd throw it away.

The sweet spot was to dash in, delight each other, and dash out, before the passion cooled and her interest was gone forever. To please her, while he could.

Which meant the time to reunite with Lady Dawn was now or never.

As he scanned the teeming crowd in search of her, his gaze lit upon a different familiar face: Mr. Alsop. Perfect! Mr. Alsop would know who she was. Lady Dawn had mentioned him by name. In fact, that was a clue to her identity in and of itself. Any woman who scheduled appointments with her lovers starting at the ungodly hour of ten a.m. could only belong to one profession.

Lady Dawn was a courtesan.

The realization did not bother Reuben in the least. He had never needed to pay for female attention before, but he was happy to make an exception in this case, if it meant finally making love to Lady Dawn. Just once, to get it out of his system.

He edged his way through the crowd to Mr. Alsop. "Alsop, my boy, how do you do? I'm looking for a woman."

Alsop snorted. "When are you not?"

"Ha ha, so witty. In this case, she's an acquaintance of yours. I'm hoping you can point me in the right direction."

"What's her name?"

"That's the thing. She failed to give it."

"One of your many nameless lovers, I presume?"

"Not yet. That's what I'm hoping to remedy. She's absolutely gorgeous... I think. Her hair is brown... or red... or gray. Somewhere between blond and black. She was white...ish. Possibly tan, I couldn't really tell. Voluptuous, yes. Truly a marvelous bosom, though I'd wager she can't weigh more than... Short! She's very short. I'd be shocked if she came up to your nipples."

"Now, see here." Mr. Alsop's eyes narrowed. "What kind of game is this?"

"Game?"

"Hair you can't recall if its brown or red or gray? Abominably short of stature? You're after a nondescript woman the size of a troll. We both know I know *exactly* who you're talking about, and I won't have you interfering with my plans."

"No, no," Reuben said earnestly. "I'm very clear on your schedule, and won't be interrupting your bit at all, I promise."

Alsop frowned. "Then what can you want with my fiancée?"

Ice frosted Reuben's veins.

"With your... What was that?" he managed faintly.

Alsop gestured across the room toward a wall of wallflowers whose presence Reuben hadn't even registered.

There, in the middle of their midst, was Lady Dawn. As it turned out, there'd been enough starlight to recognize her heart-shaped face after all. Or maybe it was the complete disarray of her chestnut hair, thanks to Reuben's hands. Lady Dawn was not looking his way, but rather was deep in conversation with some tall blond chit holding a plate piled with cakes.

It made no sense whatsoever.

"Your... fiancée?" Reuben repeated blankly.

"Our betrothal isn't official yet," Alsop admitted. "A few hours ago, she gave me permission to call upon her father in the morning. I'll sign the marriage contract then. I'd rather wed the sister, but I can't turn down that dowry."

Dowry.

Marriage contract.

Lady Dawn hadn't wished to fornicate. She was here to find a husband. And *found* one. And then believed Reuben to be the better catch.

When she'd said to drop by before ten a.m. to beat the competition, she didn't mean she was squeezing him in for an assignation. She meant, come prepared to make an offer of marriage.

Alsop crossed his arms. "What do *you* want with her?"

"Nothing," Reuben gasped.

Lady Dawn hadn't been playing a role. She *was* a nubile, virginal wallflower. No doubt from exactly the sort of upstanding, well-connected society family Reuben avoided at all costs.

From her perspective, Reuben—a society gentleman from a famously prominent family—had just compromised the ever-loving kittens out of her. By the rules of polite society, and by her obvious air of *I-just-came-from-an-illicit-tryst*, her reputation was now ruined.

In order to save her, Reuben was obligated to propose.

Parson's trap. Leg-shackled. Game over.

"I'd rather die," he whispered in horror.

"Ugh, I know," said Mr. Alsop. "The homely

wife I could do without. It's the tract of land I really want. Three generations ago, that family and mine shared an adjoining—"

He launched into a completely unnecessary speech on Welsh property law that Reuben tuned out entirely.

All was not lost. The good news was, no one *knew* Reuben had compromised Lady Dawn. They'd stopped short of consummation—thank God—which meant his streak of never debauching a virgin was still fully intact. He supposed he ought to at least talk to her and clear up the confusion, but why insert himself further in a situation that was never meant to involve him in the first place?

As a wallflower, Lady Dawn was garnering little to no attention, which meant it was possible no one would notice her flushed cheeks and tangled hair and wrinkled gown and draw the obvious conclusion.

The final piece of good fortune was that she didn't *need* Reuben to offer for her. She already had someone who wanted her—or wanted her land, anyway—and would be officially and irrevocably betrothed by ten a.m. tomorrow morning, thereby securing her reputation. Anyone who did happen to recall seeing a few hairs out of place would simply assume the happy couple had anticipated their vows.

The icing on top was that Lady Dawn had explicitly given Alsop permission to marry her. Reuben wasn't callously abandoning her to her fate. He was letting her seek her destiny with a man who actually wanted to be married. Or was at least willing to visit the parson, in any case.

The disastrous situation was turning out perfectly. Lady Dawn would become Mrs. Alsop, and Reuben could remain a rake until infinity.

And he would never, ever make a mistake like that again.

"Congratulations," he said the moment Alsop paused his boring monologue to take a breath. Reuben gave him a hearty clap on the shoulder. "Lucky man. You're doing the right thing."

Before Alsop could respond, Reuben hurried from the ballroom, allowing no one to waylay him.

That was it. His final appearance in polite society. He would never again risk stumbling into a romantic interlude with some marriage-minded debutante.

Reuben was a bachelor who liked it that way. He would remain single until the day he died. By staying out of polite society's way, he needn't fear running across Lady Dawn again. Hell, he didn't even know her real name. Which would change soon anyway. He made a mental note to avoid the entire Alsop family in the future. The entire ton, while he was at it.

And as for his still uncomfortable breeches after his foiled romantic tryst with Lady Dawn... Well. He would forget her soon enough.

Reuben would make sure of it.

CHAPTER 4

*G*ladys sat in the center of a small sofa, squeezed between her mother and sister. The only other piece of furniture of note in the miniature parlor of their rented guest quarters was a single armchair, in which sat Gladys's father.

She was not at all certain where Mr. Medford was supposed to sit when he arrived, but she supposed they'd sort it out then, along with everything else. Gladys had joyfully informed her family that a proposal would be imminent, but she had not yet shared Reuben Medford's name. She wanted the unanticipated catch to surprise and delight them, just as it had her.

"You're sure this mystery caller is coming?" fretted her mother.

"*Yes,*" Gladys said firmly. "Before ten. We were clear on that point."

It was currently half-past nine. Her family had been scrunched into the parlor since nine, none of them willing to miss an event as momentous as this. Despite the close quarters, Gladys supposed she was lucky that their rented rooms had a parlor at all.

"Kitty acquitted herself well last night," said Mother. "Danced every set but two."

Kitty had also danced twice with Mr. Alsop, not that Gladys cared. She might have been hurt or jealous if it had happened before she'd met Mr. Medford, but now she needn't settle for a mismatch like Mr. Alsop at all. She hadn't told her family about *his* offer, either. Or that he'd seemed more interested in her sister.

"Kitty danced almost every set," said Father, "but no marriage offers?"

"It was her first evening out!" Mother scolded him.

It was also a harbinger, and they all knew it. If even effervescent Kitty with her sunny personality and beautiful blond looks couldn't snare a suitor at a matchmaking festival, then it was up to Gladys to provide her baby sister with the one thing she lacked: a dowry.

Gladys had it all worked out. Her first act as the new Mrs. Medford would be to convince her husband to sell the Welsh property to Mr. Alsop for twice the price it was worth, then donate half of the sum to Kitty in the form of a dowry. In that manner, Kitty would enter her first season with the same financial advantages Gladys had been afforded, and Medford would still have a windfall commensurate with the value of the plot of land.

She was certain she could convince him. Medford hadn't asked a single question about the land at all. She doubted he even knew it was her dowry. A man as wealthy as he was would look upon such details as incidental. He didn't care about Wales.

He cared about Gladys's breasts. Property she was happy to give him, whenever he wished.

"Well," said Kitty. "It's nine forty-five."

"He'll be here," said Gladys.

They all looked at the clock upon the mantel, which was much better than all of them staring at Gladys. She'd barely been able to keep a blush from staining her cheeks all morning.

That was the other reason she hadn't mentioned Mr. Medford's name. If they got that out of her, they'd want to know how she had met him. Neither of her parents had made the introduction, and no one else in the ballroom knew Gladys's name.

"I kissed him in the garden" was far too scandalous to ever admit. She hoped Mr. Medford had come up with a plausible alternative explanation. Gladys didn't wish to accidentally contradict his story by inventing one of her own.

She sent another look at the clock. Nine fifty. Nerves prickled beneath her skin. Where *was* he?

She wished she'd written down her address for Mr. Medford, but he must know where to find her. Blushing Maid Inn was one of the biggest and best in Marrywell, which meant Mr. Medford was probably staying under this very roof himself.

And there was no need to remind him of her name. She'd told him herself, from the close distance of *right there on his lap*, to which announcement he'd answered, "I know."

In addition, they'd been treated to both Mother and Kitty screaming *Gladys Bell! Gladys Maria Bell!* from the open door.

More importantly, Mr. Medford had known who Gladys was even *before* she spied him in the garden. He'd specifically said he'd been desperate to kiss her all night. And promised to come to her hotel room on the morrow. He'd gone so far as to say he felt as though he'd been waiting for her all his life.

A man *that* much in love would be here before ten. She was sure of it.

Granted, she'd also been sure that he would come and pluck her from the wallflower wall for a dance. She'd stood there all night, looking as approachable as she could, but she never saw him again. He must have been called away for some reason. She would ask for a full explanation when he arrived.

Gladys straightened her spine. She was about to become the bride of someone who *wanted* to spend time with her. Who wanted to kiss her, not assume control of her land. If Gladys had to beget heirs, she'd rather it be with a man who made the act a pleasure. Who actually *wished* to make love to her. Who looked at her and saw passion, not a property.

"It's ten," said Kitty.

"I said he'll be here. Don't worry."

But ten turned into ten-oh-five, then ten fifteen, then ten thirty. At ten forty-five, there was still no sign of Reuben Medford. There was no sign of anyone.

Father sighed and lowered his newspaper. "I see you've made me waste my morning."

"*Wait*," Gladys begged. "Just a few more moments. He's... He's a late riser."

That's what it was. He had been horrified at the thought of paying a call at ten a.m. rather than ten p.m. Perhaps he'd overslept. Or worse—what if something had happened to him? Had he succumbed to an accident on his way back to the inn? Or taken ill?

"Eleven," said Kitty.

A knock sounded on the door.

"Oh, thank God," Gladys muttered.

She leapt to her feet, then second-guessed herself. Was she supposed to remain seated? Or, given the size of the parlor, was it best for them all to mill about on foot rather than demonstrate the lack of sufficient seating?

"I'll get it," said Mother.

Father harrumphed and set down his paper.

Gladys pinched her cheeks and plumped her bosom as surreptitiously as she could.

"How do I look?" she whispered to Kitty.

"Beautiful," answered Kitty. "Like you always do."

Only a sister would think so was Gladys's usual rejoinder, but for once, it was no longer true. Handsome Reuben Medford found Gladys desirable. In his arms, she'd actually *felt* beautiful for the first time in her life.

"Oh!" Mother exclaimed through the cracked door. "It's you!"

Gladys beamed.

Mother opened the door fully and stepped aside. Mr. Alsop stepped into the room.

Gladys's heart bottomed. She took an involuntary step backwards and tripped onto the sofa cushion with a *whoosh*.

"I've come to speak to Mr. Bell, if I could please," said Mr. Alsop.

Father rose to his feet and tossed his rolled newspaper onto the armchair. "About which of my daughters?"

Mr. Alsop's eyes passed over Gladys to rest longingly on Kitty. It was not Kitty's fault. She could not help her beauty any more than Gladys could help her plainness. Gladys had just hoped that today, at least, just for a moment... *she* could be the important one.

Alsop wrested his gaze back to their father, then swallowed and said, "The eldest, sir."

Gladys clenched her fists. It had been the wrong question. Alsop wasn't here for her at all. He wanted the Welsh land at all costs. She was right to think Medford ought to double the price. Perhaps even triple it.

Mr. Medford hadn't made her feel like a pile of dirt that came along with the castle. As soon as he arrived as promised, he'd make her forget absolutely everything except being in his arms.

"This is a wonderful surprise," gushed Mother, sending congratulatory glances toward Gladys.

"Not that much of a surprise," said Father, holding out his hand to shake Mr. Alsop's. "Am I wrong to suppose a certain property in Wales factored into your decision making?"

"*Rupert!*" Mother scolded him. "The girls are *right here.*"

Neither one of which was a stranger to how aristocratic marriage marts were supposed to work: Exactly like this. Gladys swallowed her humiliation.

"Marrywell was supposed to be different," Kitty whispered. "This festival makes love matches."

"Mine will be here any moment," Gladys said with significantly less confidence than she felt.

Mr. Medford must have fallen ill. Or broken his ankle. Or rushed home to aid his ailing mother.

"If I'd known you were coming, I would have drawn up a contract," said Father.

Mr. Alsop cast an irritated glance toward Gladys. "One might have expected you'd alert your father to expect me. Seeing as you gave your permission twelve hours ago—"

"I rescind it," said Gladys.

"*What?*" everyone else in the room gasped in unison.

Kitty looked shocked. Mother looked horrified. Father looked confused.

And Mr. Alsop looked absolutely furious. "You cannot rescind it."

"I just did." Panic and exhilaration warred within her. She had never stood up to her parents before. Never imagined turning down a suitor, even one like Mr. Alsop. But Mr. Medford had said he would be here. Gladys couldn't accept a miserable existence with Alsop when she could have a wonderful one with Medford—and provide ever so much better for her sister and mother, as well. Marrying Mr. Medford was the best path for all of them.

Gladys jumped to her feet and stood tall. "I shan't marry you."

Mr. Alsop turned to Father and said tightly, "If you would please inform your recalcitrant child—"

Was *that* any way to court a bride?

"I'm not a child. I'm twenty-one, which means I needn't marry you if I don't want to, and I. Do not. Want to." Gladys enunciated each word.

Mr. Alsop spun back to her father. "Sell me the property. I'll pay ten percent more than my previous best offer."

"I'm sorry," Father answered. "I promised my daughter a dowry."

"But if she won't let anyone *have* it…" Alsop let out an aggrieved huff, spun on his heels, and stormed out through the door before anyone could stop him.

Not that Gladys wished to prolong his visit.

Mother turned toward Gladys. "What on earth has got into you? That's not only the sole offer you've ever had, but also the best one you're likely to get. Go after him!"

"I shall not."

"*Why* not?"

"Someone else has won my heart," Gladys admitted.

"Then where the devil is he?" Father asked in bewilderment.

"He'll be here... soon," she promised.

And then waited all morning.

All afternoon.

All evening.

All night.

CHAPTER 5

*W*hen the following dawn came and went with no sign of Mr. Medford, not a glimpse or a note or even a whisper, Gladys had to face the truth:

He wasn't coming.

"Stop moping around the parlor," Mother said with a sigh. "We've matchmaking events to attend. There's to be a balloon launch in the botanical gardens. The pre-launch picnic begins in one hour."

Gardens. The botanical gardens weren't the same garden in which Gladys had kissed Mr. Medford—and more—but perhaps that was where she could find him.

"I'll get my bonnet," she said, and hurried to do just that.

The inn was a ten-minute walk from the gardens, or would have been if everyone else in Marrywell weren't clogging the main road. At least the traffic was all moving in the same direction: toward the botanical gardens.

A series of ropes on posts cordoned off the area from which the balloon would launch. Most of the picnickers had spread their blankets nearby, for the best view.

Gladys was so intent on scanning the crowd for Mr. Medford's face that it took several long moments and a strange creeping sensation before she realized many of the women in the crowd... were looking back at *her*.

Odd. Her brow furrowed. Was it because there was no convenient wall to hide wallflowers here in the garden? Was she meant to stand against the hedgerows instead of shake out a picnic blanket with her family?

Oh, *family*. That was it. They weren't looking at Gladys. They were looking at her younger sister. Kitty's stunning beauty always caught people unawares and caused a second, third, or tenth look. Nothing out of the ordinary with that.

Gladys ignored the stares and returned to searching for Mr. Medford. She couldn't find him. Not from this picnic blanket, anyway.

"Mother, Father, I'll be back soon." She scrambled to her feet.

Mother looked up from the open basket. "Where are you going?"

"I... see someone." Many someones. Thousands of them. Just not the man she was looking for. Gladys hurried off before her mother could ask more questions.

She looked for Mr. Medford in every corner. Behind every bush and tree. In every group. On every blanket.

"On the hunt, are you?" cackled an older woman, lifting a flask in salute.

Gladys frowned and hurried on. She caught sight of one of the fellow wallflowers she'd spoken with two nights earlier at the ball.

"My apologies for the interruption," she said in a rush. "I'd wondered if you'd seen... the, er, gentleman we discussed the other night."

The wallflower snorted. "Not lately, but we all know why."

"*I* haven't a clue," Gladys said in bewilderment. "Do be so kind as to tell me."

"Haven't you heard?"

Her heart stopped. "Is he hurt? Sick? Attending to familial duty?"

"In the best condition of his life, from the sound of it. He's always been an absolutely shameless rake—"

"He has?" Gladys managed faintly. But Mother had sworn all gentlemen present were on the hunt for a bride!

"—and for the last two days, he's had a different woman on his arm every time he's been spotted."

"Spotted *where*? I've not been able to find him."

"And you won't. Not if you're looking *here*. He's been seen emerging from the private hotel rooms of half a dozen notoriously fast women in the past twenty-four hours alone. By now, he's up to number seven or eight. Who knows when that rakehell finds time to sleep!"

Eight women in a single day. No wonder Mr. Medford hadn't found her. He wasn't *looking* for her. Nor would he be. He was a conscienceless libertine, driven by lust alone. He didn't care about *her*. The closest warm body would suffice. Gladys was simply one more handkerchief to use and discard, from a bottomless trough of waiting linen.

Last night, after their kiss, whilst she was vibrating nervously against the wainscoting, waiting for him to come and ask her to dance... he was already off with someone else.

And then someone else, and someone else, and someone else.

He was entertaining himself with an endless parade of women, none of which were Gladys. It would never be Gladys. He'd already moved on to brighter flowers.

But he hadn't just kissed her. He'd helped himself to her breasts. Compromised the absolute potatoes out of her. And had no intent to do the gentlemanly thing and save her reputation. He'd treated her as though she was a whore. As if she was disposable. As if she didn't matter.

Because Gladys *didn't* matter. Not to Mr. Medford. Not to anyone.

That wasn't passion she'd experienced in his arms. It wasn't even pity. It was *boredom*. Convenience. Something to do to pass the time, and then immediately forget all about.

"Thank you for letting me know," Gladys managed.

She trudged back to her parents' picnic blanket and took a seat next to her sister. No sooner had Gladys settled into place, than a pinch-faced woman approached their family with her index finger outstretched.

"I cannot believe you would dare to show your face in public!"

Gladys gaped up at her. The woman was definitely pointing her finger at Gladys, and not Kitty. The manicured nail was mere inches from Gladys's nose.

"Me?" she asked anyway.

The woman swung her finger toward Kitty, and her gaze toward Gladys's parents. "I'm surprised an upstanding family like yours would allow the

56

youngest daughter, so full of potential, anywhere near your trollop of an elder daughter."

"Trollop?" Mother repeated in bafflement. "*Gladys?*"

"Don't let her innocent looks fool you," said the older woman. "I wasn't the only one to see her sneak in from the garden with leaves in her hair and her dress askew."

The entire wide-eyed family swiveled their heads toward Gladys in surprise.

Gladys's face immediately flamed with heat.

"It's *true?*" Mother said in disbelief.

"My entire sewing circle saw her," the woman said in triumph. "We separated at once to spread the word, so that no honorable gentleman is taken in by this trollop's virginal-looking face. I hope she knows better than to show herself in polite society again."

With that, the woman stalked away.

The Bell family stared at Gladys in shock.

"I..." she managed, then hung her head. "I'm sorry."

"You're *ruined*," Kitty whispered in panic. "What do we do now?"

"We... We..." Mother sucked in a deep breath. "We must distance ourselves from her at once."

"Distance yourselves?" Gladys repeated. "From *me?*"

"You turned twenty-one last month," Father said slowly. "You have your majority."

"And... you ruined your own reputation with your actions." Mother took Kitty's hand. "We cannot allow your proximity to ruin your sister's bright future as well."

"But—but I have no other home," Gladys stammered. "No income! No other family. No options."

"I suggest you take your complaints to whomever you had your tryst with," Father said coldly.

"I can't *find* him," she blurted out.

Father looked unmoved. Mother looked distraught, but resolute. And Kitty: terrified. All three of them leaned away from Gladys. They were already distancing themselves from her.

Her stomach roiled. The strange looks from random picnickers now made sense. And if all of these people knew Gladys was ruined because of a tryst in the garden, then Reuben Medford knew it, too.

He had known the risks when he had yanked Gladys behind the hedgerow and kissed her, uninvited. He was the one who had destroyed her reputation, and he was the only one with the power to save it. But he wasn't here. He was *never* coming for her. Under any circumstances.

Because nothing would happen to *him*.

Instead of taking responsibility for his role in this disaster, Mr. Medford chose to abandon Gladys to unimaginable consequences whilst he flitted about carefree. Likely off ruining some other girl, whilst a thousand accusing eyes glared at Gladys instead of the balloon launch.

But she hadn't done this alone.

"It was Reuben Medford," she said in a rush. "He... He grabbed me and kissed me, out of nowhere. He said he'd been planning it all night. When I heard you calling, I ran away before his seduction could go further."

Her family's eyes were pitying.

"Oh, darling. I know a rakehell makes for an easy scapegoat," said her mother, "and the heir to a viscountcy would be an envious husband to land.

But you cannot really believe anyone would think that a popular, handsome gentleman who could have his pick of the entire ton would instead choose—"

You.

The word went unsaid. It was unnecessary. Gladys could shout Reuben Medford's name from the rooftops, and no one would believe her. Not even her own parents.

"You must go now," Mother whispered. "Your presence is causing a scene."

"Go *where?*" Gladys asked desperately.

"Anywhere but here," Father answered. He wrapped his arm about Kitty's slender shoulders. "I'm sorry, Gladys. You've left us no choice. From this moment on, we have only one daughter."

She cast her frantic gaze toward her sister. Kitty's horrified eyes were wet with tears, but she made no attempt to stop her elder sister from rising from the picnic blanket. Devastated, Gladys pushed herself up with shaking limbs. The entire world seemed to be tilting off its axis. She had an entire life to live, and only four shillings in her reticule. What was she to do now?

Even if she *could* find Mr. Medford, it was clear he had no intention of lifting a finger to help her, much less make an honest woman of her by marrying her himself. He was no gentleman. He was a heartless rake and a despicable user of women.

Reuben Medford hadn't just cost Gladys her home, and any hope of a happy future. He'd made her lose her entire family.

She would never forgive him.

CHAPTER 6

Five years later
Marrywell, England
1817 May Day Matchmaking Festival

ladys's hackney rolled to a stop in front of the Blushing Maid Inn. Carriages lined the pedestrian-filled street. The annual matchmaking festival was once again underway.

She could scarcely believe she was back in Marrywell after all these years. She'd chosen to reserve lodgings at the same inn as before—it was, after all, one of the best hotels in town—but of course, nothing else in her life was the same as back then.

She was five years older, for one. Six-and-twenty now. Her face had lost most of its youthful roundness, leaving her with high cheekbones and a more angular countenance. She hadn't grown any taller, but she knew how to wear clothing that accentuated her curvaceous figure. Instead of bland and plump, she looked elegant and alluring.

"Here you are." Gladys handed the driver his

fare, and an extra vail for ferrying her all the way from London.

He scrambled out of the carriage to hold the door open for her. "It was my pleasure."

She took his arm and floated to the ground, the flowing silk of her skirts hiding the elevated heel of her boots.

The hotel porter rushed forward to collect her trunks from the carriage. There would be a vail in it for him, too, though that was not why he had abandoned his other guests in order to prioritize Gladys.

It was the almost undetectable cosmetics, and the way the celestial blue silk clung to her bosom and hips that had done that.

"Thank you," she murmured in her habitual throaty voice.

That was new, too. Or had been, once. It was now second nature. As was the careless way she lifted her face and threw back her shoulders, sashaying into the reception area with a straight spine and hips swaying seductively.

"Mary Smith," she told the proprietor. "I have a reservation."

"Of—of course." He was almost too flustered by the view down her bosom to remember to take down her name. He fumbled the key twice before he managed to place it in her gloved palm.

"Thank you," she purred.

"If you need anything at all," he blurted. "Anything."

She smiled and spun away, motioning for the porter to follow her up the stairs with her trunks.

Apartment number twelve. The same suite as before. This time, she was checking in without her family. The old hurt was hollow now, and not as fresh. She had returned on her own terms, and on her own two feet.

And what were those terms, precisely? Simple. Gladys was here for one reason only:

To find Reuben Medford and make him pay.

He had all but disappeared from the beau monde after ruining Gladys. She wasn't welcome in those circles anyway, but she'd entertained enough aristocrats to have heard Medford's name from time to time.

His careless treatment of a desperate, naïve wallflower had cost Gladys everything, and Medford nothing. Not only did he suffer no consequences for his actions, by all accounts, the cad had become an even worse rakehell than before. God only knew how many other foolishly hopeful women he had ruined over the years. *Someone* had to stop him.

And that woman was Gladys.

"Anything else, madam?" asked the porter, making no attempt to hide his interest.

"That'll be all." She handed him a shilling. "For now."

After her parents disowned her, Gladys had found herself on the street. Without references, she couldn't acquire a respectable post as a governess or a paid companion. She couldn't even get hired as a lady's maid. She lacked the experience.

Gladys could paint with watercolors and play the pianoforte, but possessed no practical skills for survival. Even a maid-of-all-work, the lowest paid of all the maid positions, where a single girl was in charge of an entire household, was well outside of Gladys's capabilities. She didn't know how to boil water, much less how to cook and clean for a family of eight.

It hadn't taken long at all to end up in the clutches of a procuress. Forced prostitution could have gone horribly wrong, but with Gladys's upper class accent and manners, she quickly attracted a wealthier sort of client. Nouveau riche men with money to spare, but without the connections required to rub shoulders with the actual beau monde. Screwing a fallen member of the ton puffed their pride… and filled Gladys's pockets.

She was now a successful courtesan with a savings account so healthy, she needn't take another client for as long as she lived. Oh, she would never live like a real princess, but she wanted for nothing. She had her own town home, staffed with a maid and a footman. Perfectly tailored gowns in the latest French fashions. A list of clients who collectively owned the biggest enterprises in all of England.

She was proud of how far she'd come. And she'd achieved it all under a pseudonym, so as not to cause pain for her family.

Not that her parents were speaking to her—or Gladys, to them. She would probably never forgive them for abandoning her at her most vulnerable. For not attempting to protect her. For always ensuring she knew she ranked last.

Her sister Kitty wrote when she could, but had to hide such correspondence from her husband, lest word get out that the esteemed Mrs. Alsop was in communication with her fallen sister—or, worse, exchanged letters with a demimondaine. When it came to reputations, Kitty now had daughters of her own to worry about.

Gladys missed her like mad, though she made a point never to be a bother. If she could make herself respectable again… But that was nothing more than a castle in the air. Given that an ordinary young woman could be ruined by a simple kiss, five years of trading sex for money was well beyond the pale.

It was not the life she would have chosen for herself. Despite the constant stream of visitors to her door, being a courtesan was as lonely as being a wallflower. The men didn't want *her*. They wanted a quick release with someone who, by definition, they needn't bother caring about.

No one knew her real name, or asked how she was doing. There was little to no conversation at all, beyond the exchange of money and jewels. A few sweaty grunts later, the door would bang shut without so much as a proper goodbye. Not that the door remained closed for long.

Gladys opened her trunk. She discarded her wrinkled traveling dress and selected a gown more suitable for a lovely spring afternoon.

She was richer than she'd dreamt of becoming, but she'd trade it all in a heartbeat if it meant her family would welcome her home. At times, she even longed to have her old life back, awkward wallflower and all. To still believe there was the possibility of *love* in her future. Or even just a moment of true connection.

That dream was long dead, but there was still one desire that kept her going day after endless day:

Revenge.

This was why she'd returned to Marrywell after all this time. After disappearing from the beau monde for half a decade, Reuben Medford had been sighted in Hampshire, near the matchmaking festival.

Now the ton's most eligible bachelor was ready

for a wife and a happy ever after? Not on Gladys's watch. There would be no blissful future for Mr. Medford until he faced his past.

This time, Gladys would not settle for a kiss. She intended to make him pay. Once she held that damnable rake's black heart in her hands... She would crush it, just as he did to her.

It didn't take long to find him. The botanical gardens' crowning jewel was an enormous hedgerow maze. Reuben Medford was holding court in a grotto at the heart, a preening cockerel surrounded by dozens of hapless clucking chicks.

He looked gorgeous, of course. At one-and-thirty, the years had only made him more handsome. His shoulders were wider, his jawline rugged, the edges of his warm brown eyes adorned with laugh lines.

Ha, ha, ha. Marvelous that he'd spent the interim years having a wonderful time. England's most prodigious rake clearly hadn't a care in the world. A self-satisfied smile and an endless buffet of tasty morsels to choose from, just like always.

From her position amongst the flowers, Gladys sensed the very moment Medford's lascivious eyes fell upon her.

He looked, looked again, then visibly collected himself.

She glanced away as if bored. Turned her back to him, as though there had been nothing at all in that grotto to interest her.

There was no need to turn around. She could feel him threading his way toward her. Excellent. Gladys allowed her lips a quick, subtle smile.

Let the games begin.

CHAPTER 7

*R*euben's heart stopped.

There she was. The woman of his dreams. Long, chestnut hair, twisted into an elegant chignon. Dark brown eyes framed by even darker lashes. Voluptuous curves, shown to perfection in a demure sunflower-yellow day dress made innocently lewd by the insistent breeze pressing against her bosom and thighs, and the backlighting of the setting sun casting the exquisite body beneath into a tantalizing silhouette.

His flesh heated and his cock stirred. All thoughts of returning to his hotel room to dive back into his history tome vanished. He wanted her. He had to have her. No one else would do. She reminded him too much of…

Of *course* this woman wasn't Lady Dawn. He knew that. Over the past five years, Reuben had done his best to avoid Alsop—easy, since the man had moved to Wales, where he'd built a stunning country estate—but nonetheless, Reuben's tortured ears had overheard countless acquaintances mention Alsop was happily married. Not just happily! Obnoxiously, boastfully, eagerly leg-shackled to a wife that...tolerated him for some reason.

It was enough to make a grown rake vomit.

But this was no time to revisit the past. Not when there was a gorgeous woman in Reuben's very near future.

Yes, yes, any time he made the mistake of attending a social gathering, he was surrounded by gorgeous women—but he wasn't interested in them. Reuben would rather be playing solitaire alone than bored in a crowd. Events like these had become excruciating. For the past five years, the women surrounding him were too blond, too tall, too ginger, too thin, too... *not* Lady Dawn.

Until today. Reuben pushed past the ladybirds flocking him, making flimsy excuses as he hurried down the grotto as quickly as his boots could carry him.

The woman had already turned away, was walking briskly, in fact, in the exact opposite direction of Reuben and the grotto.

He gave up on the walking path and cut directly across the grass, leaping over neatly trimmed geometrical flowerbeds in his hurry to reach the mystery woman's side.

She didn't even glance over at him.

"Do I know you?" he blurted out, his heart hopeful and his blood pounding.

This earned him a disinterested glance, and a blank, arched brow. "Who are you?"

"Who am..." He goggled at her, utterly speechless.

Everyone knew who Reuben Medford was! He was as famous as Beau Brummell! Even if Reuben's fame was not for the clothes he wore, but rather, for the countless dresses he took off.

For the first six-and-twenty years of his life, Reuben hadn't subscribed to a favored type. He wasn't searching for more than an attractive, willing woman. To him, all women were attractive, and plenty of them were willing, which made their mutual desires a match made in heaven.

And then came Lady Dawn.

From that day forth, he'd only been able to rouse himself for lookalikes. One after another after another, in a futile attempt to get that long-ago woman out of his system and out of his head.

None of them measured up to the real thing, and he hadn't even *had* the real thing. Look at him, running away from twenty choice offerings to chase after a siren with brown hair! Five years later, Lady Dawn was still disrupting Reuben's se-ductions just by the memory alone of a mere quarter hour that hadn't even led to a proper tumble.

It was ridiculous. It was nonsensical. And he was as powerless to resist today as he'd been that long ago night beneath the stars.

"I'm Reuben Medford," he pronounced grandly.

"Mm-hm." The interrupted woman didn't change expression or give him a second glance. Just continued on her way, her brisk steps never slowing.

Either she didn't recognize the name—Impossi-ble!—or she categorically did not care that she was standing in the presence of rake royalty. Er, *walking* in the presence. Striding humiliatingly swiftly from the presence. *Damn* it!

Was she married? There was no ring on her fin-ger, so Reuben guessed no. And she was no six-teen-year-old debutante. In her early-to-mid twenties, an unmarried woman was either a widow or a spinster, two groups that tended to throw themselves in his path, not saunter away without a backwards glance.

And this was Marrywell, for God's sake. The annual May matchmaking festival. Half of the ladies here would kill to marry him, and the other half would kill to bed him. He was the only one who could barely stomach the festivities, and would much prefer a solitary stroll beside the sea or a pretty sunset. He wouldn't even be here if his uncle hadn't ordered his presence. This time, old gray Lucifur was no longer around to make the loneliness tolerable.

At best, this Lady Dawn lookalike seemed to find *Reuben* vaguely tolerable, as if he were nothing more than a stray puppy one might pat on the head, then send along on its way.

"May I at least have your name?" he begged.

Her brows raised again. "Why?"

The question flummoxed him. "What do you mean, why? So I know what to call you."

"Will you be calling me?"

"I'd certainly like to."

"And why would that be, since you don't know me?"

"I'd like to change that, too."

A deflection, yes. But he couldn't very well say, *You remind me of the one and only woman who got away. I'd like to wrap your legs around my waist until I forget about her.*

"But why would *I* wish to know *you?*" she asked, devastatingly.

"Pause for a second and find out. Please."

"And if I'm late for an appointment with someone I do know?"

"Are you?"

"No," she admitted, pausing reluctantly. "I was out enjoying the sunshine. You have two minutes."

The memory of her silhouette against the sun still burned into his soul. "You have a pocket watch?"

Her gaze was flat. "You have one minute and fifty-five seconds."

"I'm Reuben Medford," he said again, choosing to begin anew and hoping she would allow him to come to know her a little. "I live in London. If I might be so bold, your accent suggests you're from London as well?"

She inclined her head. "I am."

There. That was something. The first concrete thing he knew about her. She lived in London, just like him. Her upper class accent and polished manners indicated she moved in the same social circles Reuben had once been an active part of.

He smiled. "If you're wondering why our paths haven't crossed before, it's because I rarely attend gatherings of the beau monde."

She gazed back at him, neither indicating she'd held any curiosity as to why they hadn't met before, nor asking any of the obvious questions, like *Why would you avoid the aristocracy?* Or, *What have you been doing instead?*

He got the distinct impression she was still counting down the seconds inside her head.

"May I accompany you through the maze?" he offered.

"What about your friends back at the grotto?"

"They…" *don't mean anything to me* was absolutely the wrong answer.

In fact, Reuben couldn't think of a *right* answer. It was as though his mystery woman had laid a verbal trap for him, which was absurd. Reuben himself had chosen to entertain his harem in the grotto. It was nobody's fault at all that this woman happened to walk past an extremely public place in the center of a celebrated landmark in the middle of a festival.

"One minute and thirty seconds," she said, as if bored.

He ground his teeth in consternation. Usually he was much smoother than this. Or rather, usually he needn't try to be smooth at all. The women he surrounded himself with didn't much care what Reuben had to say. They wanted what his body could give them, and he was happy to comply.

Being forced to impress a woman in a rapidly diminishing minute-and-a-few-seconds was dizzying and confusing. He'd never had to work this hard. If anything, he'd never had to try at all. *He* was the one who could pick and choose, who never dallied with the same woman twice, who had a waiting list a mile long.

"Are you staying for the entire festival?" he blurted out.

"I had planned to."

"Are you here to find a husband?"

"Are you here to find a wife?"

"No," he answered honestly. If she didn't know of his wicked reputation, the least he could do was set that much straight. "I've no intention to marry."

"No one has caught your eye?"

Everyone caught his eye. It was his heart that would never be caught.

And this was another of her verbal traps. If he said no, he'd seen nothing to tempt him, then that would include her. And if he said yes, and pointed out he'd nearly broken an ankle racing across the garden to meet her—then by his own admission, he had not done so for honorable, romantic reasons.

"What about you?" he asked instead.

"Still waiting for something interesting to happen," she replied. "Thirty seconds."

"At least let me know your name. That way I can greet you properly the next time we run into each other."

She hesitated, clearly weighing the merits of divulging this detail about herself. At last she gave a dainty little shrug. "Miss Smith."

He could not stop an involuntary grin from overtaking his face.

"Is my name amusing?"

"No, not at all! I'm just thrilled to learn you are Miss Smith, and not Mrs. Smith. I wasn't certain you were unmarried."

"What does it matter? I certainly won't be marrying *you*."

Reuben felt the careless rejection like a punch to his solar plexus, until he remembered *he* was the first one who had said he wasn't going to marry.

"Time's up," she said, and glanced over her shoulders with significantly more interest than she'd given him.

"Searching for something?"

"Better company," she answered dryly. "Oh look, there's a frog I haven't kissed. Maybe this time, I'll find a prince."

She strode off without another word, leaving Reuben slack-jawed and dizzy.

Her rejection was what he had always feared: that his uncle was right. Reuben wasn't just unlovable. He wasn't worth a single minute of a good woman's time.

That was why he limited himself to the wicked

ones, instead. None of *them* had ever walked away from him before he was through with her before. Well, none except Lady Dawn. He ground his teeth as the old memory washed over him anew. He couldn't subject himself to a second unrequited obsession. This time, instead of conceding defeat, he would take action.

Reuben wasn't going to let the seductive Miss Smith get away. Not without burying himself between her thighs. She might not yet *think* she wanted him, but before they were through, Reuben would make her beg for his sensual attentions.

And then he'd give her every single filthy thing she asked for.

CHAPTER 8

*S*parks of victory sizzled through Gladys's veins as she strode away from The Despicable Medford with her hips swaying.

She'd been close enough to touch and he'd been dying to do just that. It was written all over his face, in the catch of his breath, in every gesture. His wants would have to wait. The cat wasn't done playing with its mouse yet. And Medford was too cocksure about his own irresistibility to realize he was no longer directing the play.

Leaving him speechless made Gladys giddy with delight. She doubted Medford was ever caught speechless, save for when he was asleep, or had someone's tongue down his throat.

And now, no matter how many other kisses he stole, the only mouth he would be thinking about belonged to Gladys.

She had behaved more coldly toward him than she normally would with a client, though there were certainly some men who sought cruelty and more. Medford was not one of those. He didn't want to give up power. He wished to exert it. To prove his dominance, and expose women's helpless subservience to his virile masculinity, or whatever such shite he told himself whenever he glimpsed his reflection in a looking-glass.

He hadn't known what to do with Gladys, and it drove him mad. She smirked. It wasn't that a rakehell by definition always knew what to do. It was that a man as pretty as Medford had never had to *do* anything. He'd thus discovered to his shock that things were different this time. If he wanted her—and they both knew he did—he was going to have to work for it.

But it wouldn't do to be too predictable in that direction, either. The cat didn't claw at the mouse without ceasing. Sometimes, it batted the terrified little thing between its paws. And sometimes it gave the mouse a bit of space, luring it into a false sense of safety before pouncing all over again.

So Gladys threw herself into the May Day festivities. She spent the entire afternoon publicly and visibly having a wonderful time that did not involve Reuben Medford. Nuncheon, kite-flying, parade, supper, dancing. *So* much dancing.

Unlike the last time she'd been in Marrywell, Gladys stood up for every set that she wished to. Despite obviously being a spinster, there was no cringing against a wall, eyes downcast, hopes irrationally high. She simply glanced about the ballroom, made brief visual contact with her target, lowered her gaze, then raised it again, and batted her fan before her face as if the sight of him had caused a blush to rise on her cheeks. Then she turned away and waited for her mark to inevitably beg for a dance, all bumbling apologies for the impertinence of asking without a proper introduction, but unable to let her walk away without spending twenty minutes in his arms.

If only it were a trick she could easily teach the latest crop of pitiable wallflowers, huddling miserably against the drab wainscoting! But this was a skill borne of years of practice.

Though Gladys could now seduce with the barest hint of a smile, her first attempts had been godawful. But determination beget practice, and with practice came confidence, and confidence brought anything she damn well wanted.

It hadn't been an easy road. However, she had already traveled the difficult sections and had finally reached the finish. One more wee little seduction of a heartless rakehell, and she could retire to her cozy little town house with her pot of tea and her well-read library with her cat on her knees. She need never think about men—especially Reuben Medford—ever again.

In fact, she'd grown tired of tonight's dancing already. This provincial assembly room was nothing at all like the delightfully debauched soirées lords of the ton attended in search of their next mistresses.

The hour was late. Or early, depending on how one wished to look at it. Two a.m. In London, a proper party would rage at least until dawn, but out here in Hampshire, the crowd was already dwindling.

Gladys ought to return to her suite. She was restless, and wouldn't be able to fall asleep for hours, which meant she might finally reach the end of the novel she was rereading whilst she awaited its sequel.

But first, she couldn't resist a quick turn outside the ballroom. To revisit the scene of the crime, as it were.

She paused at the doorway leading to the statue

garden. It was ajar, just as it had been the fateful night she'd wandered out-of-doors for a breath of fresh air and ended up disheveled and discarded instead.

Her hand was steady as she closed her fingers about the handle and pulled open the door.

Cold night air washed over her. Crisp, dry, but chilly enough to require a shawl if one intended to be out for more than a few minutes.

She stepped outside, pulling the door almost, but not quite, closed behind her.

There was the walking path, just as she remembered it. The same statues, with new spatters of bird droppings. The same hedgerows, six feet tall and as dangerous as anything one might find in Vauxhall's Dark Paths.

But it didn't look as sordid as she recalled. If anything, it looked a little cheap. A bit plain. As though her memory had built this tiny strip of the garden into the cursed labyrinth of legendary King Minos, complete with a terrible minotaur lurking in the shadows, eager to trample any lost soul that dared to traipse past.

Gladys dared. She was not the shy, flinching creature she once was. And, though she hated herself for it, there might be a tiny spark of girlish wistfulness driving her to step off the stone walking path and across the springy grass to the shadows where she'd received her first kiss.

She'd been so surprised. So flattered. So hopeful.

Fool. Of course the handsome rake hadn't fallen in love with her at first sight. Of all the men she'd lain with over the years, not one held any interest in her beyond a series of temporary, transactional encounters.

Happily ever after didn't happen to girls like Gladys. It wasn't that lightning didn't strike twice. It would never touch her at all.

She turned away from the hedgerow without fully rounding the corner to glimpse the old stone bench, if it still stood where she remembered it. That way lay madness. There was no sense revisiting old mistakes when she had a new—

A hand closed around her wrist. She yelped as she was yanked against a tall, hard wall of man. Before she could catch her breath or her balance, his arms were around her and his mouth claimed hers.

Gladys reacted in kind out of habit—and also out of nostalgia, and hope, and surprise—until she gathered her wits enough to splay her hands on the mystery man's chest and push him far enough away to catch a moonlit glimpse of his face.

Reuben Medford.

Again.

"You," she gasped, and slammed the side of her fist against his broad chest.

He let her go in equal surprise. "You!"

"Who did you think I was?" she snapped.

"For a moment, I thought you were… Someone I… Never mind." The shifting shadows made it look as though the rake was blushing. "Forgive me my mistake. I wasn't waiting for anyone. I had intended to be alone."

"Then why did you… *Ugh.*" Gladys turned away without waiting for an answer. She didn't need one. He'd told her himself: he wasn't waiting on anyone in particular.

This wasn't a romantic nook. This was Medford's hunting ground. Five years ago, a little lost wallflower had believed their kiss to be a special moment. Had even believed, if only for a moment, that *she* was special. Instead, she was nothing more than the latest victim of a rakehell's signature lustful maneuver.

Gladys wanted a fairy tale? She was in one. And they didn't all end happily. The sculpture garden was the deep, dark forest. Medford was the iron trap, his metal jaws gaping and deadly, awaiting his prey. Any prey. It didn't matter. And she was the fluffy, innocent bunny whose gamboling pink paw happened to fall right in his path.

"You sicken me," she informed him through clenched teeth.

That wasn't the plan. She'd meant to flirt, to reel him in, to make him fall in love, and then to destroy him.

He smiled. "It didn't feel like I sickened you when you were kissing me back."

"I didn't know it was you."

"Who did you think I was?" Jealousy flashed in his eyes and tightened his voice.

Good. He might have Gladys at sixes and sevens, but Medford at least was still falling right on track.

"You shouldn't kiss a lady without permission."

"Are you a lady?"

"Are you a gentleman?"

"Not in the least. And I've never had to ask permission before." He tilted his head. "If I ask it of you, will you say yes?"

"You'll have to find out the same way everyone else does."

"May I kiss you?"

"No."

He clutched his heart as if struck by an arrow. "You are a villain. I have been desperate to see you again since the moment you left the labyrinth."

"You can barely see me in the darkness, and you couldn't see anything at all a moment ago when you were kissing me with your eyes shut."

"You watched me? Your eyes were open?"

No. Her eyes had been closed too, just as they were on that night so long ago.

Rather than answer, she raised her brows at him.

He raked a hand through his hair. "May I see you, then? *Really* see you? Somewhere with sun, or at least chandeliers?"

"I don't wish to be seen with you."

"You *don't*?"

"I have a reputation to consider." She slanted him a wry look. "Don't you? The most prolific rakehell in England, publicly wooing a random spinster. Good God, what would the gossips think?"

"I never said I planned to do any wooing."

"Then what, exactly, are you proposing?"

He stared at her in consternation, the wheels in his brain clearly spinning. "Is it still 'wooing' if both parties know their time together won't lead to matrimony?"

"Are you referring to sexual acts?" she asked archly.

He flung out his hands. "I'll pour tea for you and discuss the weather, if that's the only way you'll agree to see me."

"So you're asking what it's called when two people spend non-sexual time together in voluntary companionship. I believe the word you're looking for is 'friendship'."

"With a *woman*?" Medford said in mock horror.

Or perhaps he wasn't acting. He famously never saw the same woman twice. It did not take much imagination to realize he did not think of his conquests as friends. He didn't think of them at all.

Until now.

She inclined her head. "I will accept tea and nothing more."

"*Nothing* more?"

"Tea and conversation."

He looked appalled. "Is there never to be any hope for more?"

"There's to be no *taking* more without explicit permission. I will kiss you when and if I choose to. You'll have to earn each one… if you can."

"Then come to my hotel tomorrow afternoon." He pressed her fingers to his chest. "Everyone else will be in the assembly rooms dancing to the orchestra. You and I can have tea and conversation without any gossipy eyes spying us together."

"Which hotel?"

"Blushing Maid Inn. Do you know it? I always stay there."

Know it? Gladys always stayed there, too. Which meant, five years ago, they had indeed been under the same roof when her life fell apart as she knew it. To save her from ruin, all Medford would have had to do was walk down the corridor and knock on her door.

"Here." He pulled a calling card and a pencil out of his waistcoat pocket, scrawled something on the back of the card, then placed the small rectangle in the palm of her hand.

The moonlight was just bright enough to make out: Tea. Room Six. 5 o'clock.

She started to lower the card.

"Wait." He cupped the bottom of her hand and scribbled something else on the card.

P.M. He'd added "P.M." to the hour. Butterflies fluttered in her belly.

Her lips almost quirked at the silly inside jest before she remembered Mary Smith wouldn't know about the conversation Lady Dawn had shared with the Lord of Stars.

Gladys wasn't certain what to think about Medford remembering an idle joke from five years earlier.

Perhaps he hadn't remembered anything. More likely, specifying the exact time of day was just a peculiar quirk of his, like lying in wait behind a hedgerow in a statue garden. The coincidence meant nothing. Just like a lonely, trusting wall-flower called Gladys had meant nothing.

But all of that was about to change.

CHAPTER 9

*R*euben was preposterously nervous.

He still could not quite credit that he'd invited Miss Smith to his rented lodgings. He *never* brought women into his private space. He preferred to control the length of the encounter. To be the one who walked away.

But when she'd caught him behind the hedgerow, haunting a statue garden in the hopes of recreating that magical moment with Lady Dawn, what else could he do but hold on tight whilst he could?

Even if Lady Dawn would have materialized like an apparition in the mist, Reuben was fully aware the encounter was unlikely to end differently this time. He was still not the marrying sort. Even for Lady Dawn. But he had never stopped wishing for a few more moments of her company.

When Miss Smith had stepped into view, it had felt just like that long-ago moment. Instinctively, Reuben could not help but reenact it. For the briefest of moments, he'd even convinced himself...

But of course that was ridiculous. Miss Smith

could not be less like Lady Dawn. For one, she knew how to kiss. In the space of a heartbeat, she'd turned him inside out and left him panting for more. His heart hadn't stopped pounding in remembrance.

A soft knock sounded on the oak door.

Reuben smiled. Perfect timing. It was time for *more*.

It was five o'clock precisely. He swung the door open wide before Miss Smith could change her mind and fly away. There was no sense pretending he hadn't been standing on the other side of the threshold since half past four, in anticipation of Miss Smith's arrival.

His throat went dry at the sight of her.

Her smooth brown hair was swept up at the nape, with loose tendrils framing her pretty face. Her lips were quirked, one eyebrow arched, her dark brown eyes knowing. Her gown was at once chaste and seductive, covering everything it ought to, whilst hugging her curves and billowing sensuously about her long legs. Every inch of her looked positively delectable.

There was nothing he wanted more than to reach for her, to pull her into his embrace, to cover her mouth with his and feel her soft curves melt against him.

If he tried it, however, he was more likely to feel the sharp slap of her palm against his cheek. She would kiss him when and if she wished to, she'd warned him. And only if he'd earned it.

Reuben settled for bowing low, lifting her fingers to his lips before she could stop him, then stepping aside to welcome her into his lodgings.

The door to the bedchamber was closed, so as not to frighten her off. The entranceway doubled as a parlor. A sofa and two armchairs flanked an oval table, upon which Reuben—or, rather, the hotel maids—had laid out a gorgeous tea service.

He waited for Miss Smith to settle into an armchair before taking the one opposite her. It appeared the sofa would, for the moment, go unused. He would have much rather shared that cozy cushion with her, thigh to thigh, arm about her shoulders, yet the truth was, Miss Smith was right: The ghosts of Reuben's past might make him *believe* he shared a powerful connection with her, but they had only just met. He might be an inveterate rakehell, however, even libertines knew that the trick was taking one's time, not frighten off the prey.

"Shall I pour?" he asked.

"Allow me."

Miss Smith's elegant hands poured the tea with brisk efficiency, as though she had presided over countless such tables, in company far more illustrious than that in which she currently found herself.

Reuben once again got the impression that she was used to rubbing shoulders with the aristocracy. That perhaps this woman would not be a stranger to him now if he had bothered to attend any of the beau monde's soirées properly, rather than limit himself to lurking in its shadows.

She lifted a heavy reticule onto her lap and started to untie the string holding the large, lumpy bag together.

"Do you need something?" he asked. "There's plenty of sugar in this covered dish, and I can always ring for—"

She pulled a charmless, utilitarian hourglass

from her reticule, then placed it beside the teapot. "Now we can begin."

He stared at the hourglass. "What is that?"

"An hourglass."

"I can see that."

She stirred her tea. "Then why did you ask?"

"I meant, what is it doing?"

"Counting down the hour."

He gritted his teeth. "Why is it doing that?"

"I never give a man more than an hour of my time."

Reuben glared at the hourglass in consternation. He had finally managed to lure Miss Smith somewhere comfortable and private, and was now only to be granted sixty minutes in which to enjoy her company?

"Don't scowl so," she chided him. "It's unbecoming. Besides, proper afternoon visits between a lady and a gentleman aren't meant to last longer than twenty or thirty minutes."

"I thought we'd established that you're not a lady, and I am no gentleman," he grumbled.

"Which is why I have allotted you up to one hour." She sipped her tea. "You should be flattered."

"*Up to* an hour?" he repeated, aghast.

"You must agree that time is one's most precious resource. Once lost, it is gone forever, and cannot be regained. I take great care in determining how best to spend mine."

Oh, all right. Challenge accepted.

He smiled wolfishly. "I suppose your time must also be earned, just like your kisses?"

She fluttered her lashes at him. "Why, the gossips were wrong about you, Mr. Medford. You *do* have a working brain."

"I'm not thinking with my brain," he assured

her. "Except insofar as to strategize how I might earn acts far more scandalous than kisses."

She lifted her cup of steaming tea back to her lips, as though to hide a smile.

The deliberately provocative comment had been glib—and true—but in Miss Smith's case, Reuben found himself wishing she actually *would* see him as more than a randy rake mindlessly following his cock's every whim.

Such an uncharacteristic sentiment caught him by surprise. Seeing as he never spent more than one night in the company of any given woman, her opinion of him the next day had never signified. Reuben's conquests angled after his prick, not his personality. The entirety of those conversations could be summed up in a few dozen words—if indeed it amounted to anything more than muffled moans and gasps of pleasure.

Now that the gauntlet had been drawn, and the challenge to express himself in words rather than passionate kisses had been issued, Reuben realized he had absolutely no idea what to do.

He was absolutely, unequivocally, horrifically out of his depth.

"The weather," he blurted out. That was the ton's preferred entree into polite conversation, was it not?

Miss Smith arched a dark eyebrow. "What about it?"

"It's…" Reuben swung his head to the side to cast his gaze out of the window. "Overcast."

"Fascinating." Miss Smith cast a pointed glance toward the hourglass. "I'm so glad I paid this call, to learn something I can see with my own two eyes."

Reuben was fairly certain this was not how conversations about the weather *usually* went.

Very well, then. Non-boring conversation. Something properly interesting that she did not already know. He stared at her in frantic silence. His panicked mind had gone completely and utterly blank.

She reached for one of the biscuits on the serving tray.

"*Biscuits,*" Reuben babbled inanely.

She paused with her fingers hovering just above the plate of biscuits. "Have you something interesting to say about them?"

No. He did not. He didn't even know what flavor these were. He'd simply ordered a variety, in the hopes that one of the possibilities would meet Miss Smith's approval. That much appeared to have succeeded.

Impressing her himself, however... Still a work in progress. How the devil did the poor swains courting fashionable young ladies muddle through twenty minutes of non-sexual conversation? Especially under the watchful eye of the young lady's mother or chaperone?

No wonder they grasped at straws like *Brr, what a blustery day* and *It looks like rain.*

"This inn was built in 1534," he blurted out.

She arched her brows politely. "Was it?"

"Yes. No. The first inn on these grounds was. It burnt down twice, and has then been rebuilt in the same spot, each time slightly grander."

"Like Shakespeare's theatre?"

"Exactly like that," he said in relief. "Except the Globe Theatre burnt in 1599, then again in 1613 before being fully restored to the theatre we know in 1739. The Blushing Maid Inn likewise suffered a mishap due to a highly flammable thatched roof—"

"Presumably not due to a malfunctioning cannon during a performance of Henry VIII."

"Far more mundane, I'm afraid." He grimaced. "An incident in the kitchen."

"I'm sure it seemed anything but mundane at the time."

"You'd be right. It happened during the match-making festival. Guests were forced to seek shelter elsewhere, but there were no free rooms to be had."

"What did they do?"

"Share rooms with strangers." He wiggled his brows. "Who did not remain strangers for long."

"Making it one of the festival's greatest match-making successes?"

"The most infamous, anyway. Half of the matches that year sprang from scandal. In fact, there was a family of five daughters who—" He closed his teeth with an audible click. "I'm sorry. Two-hundred-year-old gossip is worse than the weather. I swear I don't mean to bore you."

"You're not," she replied, as though just as surprised by the realization as he was.

He recalled that she had known the fiery past of the Globe Theatre off the top of her head, as well. "Are you a student of history, too?"

She shook her head, hesitating only slightly before admitting, "Architecture."

"Which in some cases is the same thing?"

She inclined her head. "Every iron nail and wooden beam has a story."

"You like stories?"

"I love them," she said with fervor. "Even more than tea or architecture."

"You primarily read novels?" he guessed.

"Novels and newspapers and anything salacious I can get my hands on. And you... read dusty old history tomes?"

He clutched his heart. "I hang on every dusty old word."

They exchanged cautious smiles at this unexpected thread in common.

She lifted her cup. "If I'd known, I would have brought my current book. We could have made quite the cozy domestic scene."

He shook a playful finger at her. "You can read anywhere. I won't let you out of a conversation with me that easily."

"Why, Mr. Medford, I was led to believe men of your type did not care to waste time with friendly conversation."

"Men of my type?" He raised his brows. "I thought you didn't know who I was until this week."

She matched his arch look. "I may have heard a thing or two."

Indeed. Now that he recalled, hadn't she recently referred to him as the most prolific rake in all the ton? If a Londoner not knowing who Reuben Medford was when she'd first arrived at the festival was improbable, avoiding the gossip while they were both here in the same small town would be impossible.

He didn't have to wonder what tales she'd been told. The specific stories did not matter. None of his past indiscretions or the decade-long pattern of pleasure-seeking spoke particularly well of his character as a gentleman. It was no wonder Miss Smith would be skittish.

On the other hand, she now knew the truth... and had accepted his invitation anyway.

"How intriguing that, despite my sordid history, a pretty, unmarried woman should still choose to enter my private lair with no chaperone. Spending time alone with a known rake is either very brave—"

"Or very foolhardy?"

"Or a logical strategist. If neither of us are after marriage, and you are well informed of the sorts of satisfying entertainments I traditionally offer female companions... Then why, exactly, are you here, Miss Smith? Is there something I can do for you? Something... pleasurable?"

She sipped from her tea cup, her steady gaze never leaving his.

"I can clear this table with one movement," he offered. "There's also a perfectly serviceable sofa in this parlor, as well as a nice, comfortable bed on the other side of that closed door."

"I'm well aware of what you want with *me*. And as I told you..." She set her cup and saucer back on the table. "You'll have to earn it."

He reached for her hand. Slowly, to give her time to pull away. Without breaking their gaze, she allowed him to lift her soft hand in his. He brought her fingers to his lips and pressed a kiss to each one. Then he turned her hand over to expose the fluttering pulse point at her wrist. Reuben lowered his mouth to the sensitive spot. He breathed in her scent, filling his lungs with her essence, before pressing a soft kiss to the beat of her heart.

The slight catch to her breath was all the encouragement he needed.

He lifted her fingers to his own heart, drawing her closer, then cupped her cheek with his free hand and lowered his lips to hers.

The kiss was as explosive as fireworks. When

Reuben had grabbed her in the garden, he'd been reaching for a ghost of the past. He hadn't known he'd found Miss Smith instead until she'd shoved him away.

She wasn't resisting him now. She responded to his open-mouthed kisses as though she, too, felt the same insatiable hunger that was turning him inside out.

This was what he had longed for. This was precisely *who* he had needed. He hadn't known his soul was searching for Miss Smith, but now that he'd found her, Reuben was never going to—

She slipped out of his grasp and rose to her feet in one smooth movement. "Thank you for the tea, Mr. Medford. I hope you enjoy the rest of your evening."

He stared at her in shock. If she left now, Reuben was either going to have a very uncomfortable evening, or he was going to have to take matters into his own hand. Yes, yes, there were dozens or even hundreds of other willing women in Marrywell with which he could take his pleasure, but none of them were Miss Smith. Until he had her, no one else would do.

He leapt up to stop her. "Don't go. Not without one more kiss."

She ducked out of reach as she collected her reticule and her hourglass.

"Wait!" he said with surprise. "Only half the sand has fallen. It's been thirty minutes, not an hour."

"Mm-hm." She opened the door and blew him a kiss. "Try not to lose my attention next time."

The door clicked shut behind her.

After Reuben collected himself from the shock,

he darted forward and flung open the door to call her back.

The corridor was empty.

So were the stairs. He raced down them anyway. There was a clump of travelers waiting to check into the inn, but no sign of Miss Smith.

Reuben dashed outside and scanned the street in both directions. A parade of people filled the street, milling in all directions. The pink sunset streaked over the horizon. Some of the merrymakers were decked out in their best finery, clearly headed toward the assembly rooms or the garden. Others strolled toward taverns and other venues.

None of them was Miss Smith.

He let out a growl of frustration in disbelief. Most prolific rakehell in all of England? The object of his attentions had got bored and disappeared mid-kiss. Worse, Reuben *still* didn't know how to get in contact with her to beg for a second chance.

And by God, there definitely was going to be a next time. Before the end of this festival... Miss Smith *would* be in his arms.

CHAPTER 10

*G*ladys awoke earlier than was her custom back in London, but the street outside her window was already bustling with festival-goers. What time was it? She craned her neck toward the clock. Half past nine. By the size of the swelling crowd, she wouldn't be surprised to learn the merrymaking had begun anew at seven or eight o'clock.

"*A.M.*," she mumbled under her breath, then cursed herself for making a Medford-inspired jest.

She had come here in search of justice—very well, *revenge*—for the utter mess he had made of her life. Hers, and the countless other similarly naive ingenues he'd left ruined in his destructive wake over the years.

By any metric, he was the villain of the piece. She should not be chuckling to herself over his idiosyncrasies or reliving the feel of his mouth against hers. She should be plotting her vengeance. Or better yet, not thinking about Reuben Medford at all.

She'd bid farewell to her last remaining "protector" before making this journey west, which meant Gladys was *free* in a way she hadn't experienced in years. Maybe ever.

Unlike the last time she was in Marrywell, she was no wilting wallflower constrained by propriety. Gladys was a grown woman, with enough coin not to need a man. She had her independence, which was worth immeasurably more than the fiction this cursed matchmaking festival was selling.

Happy ever after? You must be jesting. Even in fairy tales, such promises of everlasting bliss were reserved solely for the prince and princess. The rest of the characters tended to suffer much darker —and, in Gladys's experience, far more realistic —horrors.

That she wished to avoid the saccharine festivities and their incessant reminders of all she had lost was no surprise. Whether she could accomplish such a feat in a small town currently swarming with half the population of England, however…

"I knew I should've brought more books," she muttered as she slipped on her pelisse.

One novel was never enough. Or it might have been, if she could manage to stop herself every night after "one more chapter". Instead, one chapter turned into two which turned into twelve, and the next thing she knew, she was on the last page and it was a quarter to three.

"Don't say it," she warned herself, but her traitorous mind had already whispered, *A.M.*

That did it. She needed to get as far away from the festival *and* Reuben Medford as possible.

She tugged her bonnet low to hide her face and headed in the opposite direction of the busy park and the pleasure gardens and the assembly rooms.

She walked and walked until the crowd thinned, then waned, then disappeared altogether.

Only then did she lift the brim of her bonnet and take stock of her surroundings. She'd walked so far that even the hotels and taverns were out of sight behind her. To her right was a smattering of sleepy cottages. To her left was a narrow dirt walking path that led into dense, leafy woods.

She chose the silent woods.

After picking her way through the forest, she came to the bank of a burbling stream. The only sounds were the rustling of leaves in the cool breeze, the occasional song of distant starlings and chiffchaffs, and the soothing gurgle of the wide, cerulean stream. It was perfect.

Her tight muscles relaxed and her spirits lifted as she inhaled the sweet scents of spring. Idly, she picked up a stone from the soil and tossed it into the water. The stone made a pleasing plop, accompanied by a sparkling series of ripples.

Smiling to herself, she glanced toward her feet in search of another rock, then sent it arcing up and into the still water.

"You're doing it wrong," came a low, male voice behind her.

Gladys gasped and spun about, one hand to her bodice. "*You.*"

Reuben Medford smiled at her. "You were expecting someone else?"

"I was expecting to be alone." She narrowed her eyes. "Were you following me?"

"If I was, I wouldn't have brought my 'dusty old history tome'," he said ruefully, lifting the large volume so she could see.

He had also come from the opposite end of the path, which meant Medford had either entered the woods via a different path, or *Gladys* was the one following in his footsteps.

So much for a moment of peace, by herself.

"I suppose you brought your novel, as well?" he asked.

"You suppose wrong." She turned her back to him. "We are not as alike as you think."

Except she *might* have brought a book, if she'd known the path was here, and she'd left herself an unread chapter or two. And they had indeed both chosen to come here, to this same bucolic woods, rather than join the throngs celebrating the May Day festivities.

"I would have thought any rakehell worth the name would have been up much too late to awaken half this early."

"Hmm." The low rumble of his voice was far too close to the back of her neck. "Thinking about how I spend my nights, are you?"

"No," she snapped. *Yes.* Constantly.

"You could join me tonight and find out."

"I'm busy."

"Well, you're not busy now, are you? Such good fortune. What better opportunity for you and I to—"

She spun around. "If you think for one moment that I have any intention of rutting with you in the dirt next to a river—"

His wide brown eyes blinked innocently. "Who said anything about pleasures of the flesh?"

She glared at him. "Then what were you referring to?"

"Teaching you to skip rocks properly, of course." He placed a smooth, flat stone in her palm, then closed his fingers around hers. "But if you'd prefer a different sort of lesson..."

"I'm happy to teach you what a rock to the head feels like."

"Skipping stones it is, then." He placed his hands on her shoulders and turned her toward the stream. "The first step is choosing the right rock. Do you feel the smooth, flat shape of the stone in your hand?"

He had taken her by surprise, that was all. That he looked as impossibly handsome in the middle of the morning as he did in the middle of the evening came as no surprise. Today, he'd left his hat behind, allowing the wind to tousle his hair, which *ought* to make him appear slovenly and disheveled, but instead merely gave him an air of youthful mischief.

Gladys was glad he could not see the consternation on her face. Reuben had her off-kilter. He'd interrupted her peaceful morning, and instead of lashing out... she had a stone in her hand, and *his* hands on her hips.

She had not meant to let him touch her. Not yet. She'd plotted every step of her seduction-then-public-rejection, and he had not yet earned curve-touching privileges.

Then again, now that they were clear that there would be no illicit liaison here on the bank of the stream, perhaps this was a perfect time to allow him to feel as though his seduction of *her* was going to plan.

"All right," she said. "What do I do now?"

She could *feel* him smile behind her. He thought he had won. How precious.

Gladys would *never* fall for a rakehell such as Medford. Not again. He'd destroyed that hopeful, romantic part of her years ago. Now he would learn what that sensation felt like.

It was her turn to lift his hopes, then break his heart.

Medford wouldn't be socially ruined, as Gladys had been. Or have his entire life incontrovertibly shattered, as he'd done to Gladys. But by God, for once there would be consequences to his thoughtless dalliances.

Enough pain so that *next* time, maybe he'd think about the human being he was playing with.

"Now." His soft voice fluttered behind her ear. "We're not going to toss the stone up into the air, as you were doing before. The trick is to cast it straight and true."

She tensed, certain that he was going to close his hand about hers once more. Dreading it. Dying for it. Yearning to feel her fist swallowed up in the strength of his hand.

"Ready?" His hand closed about hers. She shivered. He drew her fist back slightly. "Loosen your grip."

Loosen? She was so weak, she was practically boneless. She was lucky she was holding herself upright, and not nestling backwards into his warm chest. If that made it difficult to release her death grip on this rock, well, that was because she'd learnt the importance of self-preservation the hard way. He was a much better teacher than he realized. He'd taught her not to trust *him*. No matter what love words he might utter or how pleasurable his rakish touch might feel.

"Now I throw?" she managed, her voice unaccountably strained and breathy.

"Now you throw."

She chucked the stone into the water and spun out of his grasp before he could muddle her thoughts any more.

"Not like that," he said, as though she really had invited him out here to give her lessons on skipping rocks. "Watch me do it."

She crossed her arms from a safe distance.

He scanned the earth for appropriate stones, selecting three before straightening. He showed her each one, then assumed a sturdy position, his wide shoulders facing the stream. "Are you watching?"

"Riveted," she said dryly.

He tossed the stone several inches into the air, catching it lightly, then drew his arm back and sent the stone spinning forward, to skip twice across the stream before sinking into the water.

"I am agog at your prowess," she told him. "This must be how it felt to watch Michelangelo paint the Sistine Chapel."

"I can do better," he assured her. "Watch this."

This time, the stone skipped four times before disappearing into the water.

Grinning, he turned to her and made a come-hither motion with his hands, whilst wiggling his eyebrows provocatively. "Return to my embrace, sweet protégée. I shall not rest until I've taught you the right moves."

"You intend to manhandle me until I can skip a rock across a river?"

"I shan't leave your side until you have the knack of it."

She held out her hand. "Rock."

He placed the third and final stone in her palm.

She turned toward the spring and let fly with a practiced motion.

The stone skipped nine times before sinking.

Gladys wiggled her fingers at the astonished

rake. "Au revoir, Mr. Medford. Do have a lovely day."

"But," he sputtered. "You... How did you *do* that?"

"It's all in the wrist. I'm sure you can find someone to teach you."

"But how did... When I came around the corner, you were..."

"...not trying to skip stones," she said wryly. "I was performing an advanced technique known as 'throwing rocks into a river because I felt like it and wanted to be alone'."

"You allowed me to give you a completely unnecessary and unhelpful lesson."

"You forced your unsolicited lesson upon me, so certain were you of your superior skill and wisdom in the face of my regrettable female inferiority."

"I..." His cheeks flushed. "I deserve that. You're right. You didn't ask for my help, or even suggest that you were *trying* to skip stones. I knew you hadn't come to the woods in search of my company, and I forced it upon you anyway. I'm sorry. It was not well done of me."

Gladys glared at him. Damn Reuben Medford and his pretty apology! She hadn't known he even knew the words *I'm sorry*, much less would be man enough to use them.

"I don't suppose you'd show me the trick of it?" he queried.

To refuse now would be churlish. Not to mention counterproductive. She was trying to reel him in, not spur him away.

"Very well." She uncrossed her arms and let them fall to her sides. "Find a rock."

He immediately set to searching for stones,

then brandished five of them proudly, as if presenting her with a bouquet of flowers.

She plucked one from the pile. "Watch carefully."

Narrating each of her slow, exaggerated movements, she assumed her favored stance, explained the motion of her arm and the grip on the stone, then sent it flying down the stream.

It skipped thirteen times.

Was she showing off? Definitely.

"You *are* the Michelangelo of stone-skipping," he said, awestruck. "All right, my turn. Is my wrist in the right position?"

"You're throwing a stone, not—" *stroking your cock.* The words crumpled into a cough in her throat.

Gladys the high-priced courtesan might make lewd jests of that nature, but "Miss Mary Smith" was... well, perhaps not *proper*, but certainly conservative enough not to lift her skirt to a rake like Medford without credible assurance that he was fully and truly in love.

"I'll show you," she murmured, and cupped her hand around his. Her bosom pressed into his back, and her skirts fluttered around his legs.

"I've already forgotten everything," he said hoarsely. "Can I kiss you instead?"

"Earn it," she whispered into the back of his neck. "Seven skips, and you can have a kiss."

There had never been a more determined student.

Medford flung rocks into the spring as though firing arrows from a full quiver. The first two sank unceremoniously. The next skipped two, then three times, respectively. He visibly forced himself to take stock of his surroundings and his stance, then tried again.

Five skips this time.

He spun to face her, his eyes shining triumphantly. "Closer."

She blew on her fingernails, as if bored. "Not close enough for a kiss."

He collected a new batch of stones. His face was a furious mask of concentration as he set about trying to copy her stance and her throw.

Four skips. Five. Six. Two. *Seven.*

He let out a war whoop and swung her in a euphoric circle.

She could not help but laugh along with his infectious joy.

Rather than put her down, he gathered her close, and covered her mouth with his.

This was not a kiss of seduction. This was a kiss of triumph, of teamwork, of relief, surprise, and success. Which made it all the more seductive. This kiss was not something he was doing *to* her, but rather sharing *with* her. A kiss that was neither his nor hers, but *theirs*. A celebration of what they could accomplish when working together.

And if the man could kiss like this... Gladys could only imagine what making love to him must be like.

Coupling, she corrected herself firmly. Rutting, screwing, anything but making love. This was one of his tricks: making her think gentle "feelings" had anything to do with the matter. He couldn't even remember the names of his past conquests. He certainly hadn't loved them. And he didn't love Gladys, either.

Not yet. But he would. And then she would break his heart.

"How did you learn to skip rocks like that?" he murmured against her lips.

How? By accident. *Why* and *when* were better questions.

The reason she'd learned to skip rocks was because, after she was ruined and banished, escaping into the privacy and beauty of nature was one of the few moments of idle pleasure a penniless vagabond could give herself.

Gladys hadn't learned to skip rocks out of any particular love of rocks. She'd learned out of necessity. During a dark time when no one she cared about would give her the time of day, and she couldn't bear to couple with one more sweating lecher for a shilling.

All thanks to Reuben Medford.

"Natural born talent, I guess," she said lightly, and pushed out of his embrace. "Now, if you'll excuse me..."

"Tell me how to reach you," he blurted. "Where are you staying?"

She arched a brow in silence.

"Haven't earned that yet," he guessed correctly, with a sheepish smile. "How about your first name? You've certainly earned mine. I've no wish to be 'Mr. Medford' to you. Please say you'll call me Reuben."

She paused, lips pressed together, then nodded.

"And yours?" he coaxed, taking her hands in his. "Please?"

Her mouth opened. She meant to tell him *Mary*, truly she did, but what came out of her mouth was, "Gladys."

A foolhardy risk. She'd told him her name before. He'd heard it multiple times that first night. Before she was ruined, back when she still had her family's love, and dreams of love and a first kiss. If Medford finally put two and two together...

But no. There was no flicker of recognition in his lust-struck eyes. He didn't remember her name, just like he hadn't remembered her face. She was just a woman who hadn't yet agreed to lie with him. A future conquest to be won and discarded. No more, no less.

"Gladys," he purred in his best seductive-rake voice. "A beautiful name for a beautiful woman."

Why, yes it was beautiful. Gladys's mother had given that name to her.

And *this* time, Reuben Medford was going to remember it.

CHAPTER 11

$\mathcal{T}$he next morning, Reuben leapt out of bed unconscionably early, made himself as dapper as possible, then set out in search of Gladys.

His mission did not go well.

Despite haunting all the places he'd glimpsed her previously—the secluded bench behind the assembly rooms, the hedgerow labyrinth inside the botanical gardens, the river where they'd skipped rocks—she was nowhere to be seen.

As much as he disdained the festival's legitimate planned activities—a committed rake like Reuben had no intention of finding himself leg-shackled to a wife, and therefore saw no reason to string along women who were the opposite of what he was looking for—Reuben eventually had no choice but to put in an appearance at those events as well, in the hopes of seeing Gladys again.

She wasn't at any of those, either.

He ground his teeth in frustration as he was forced to make flirtatious smiles and flimsy excuses to the pretty debutantes that clogged his path.

He'd come to this festival because his uncle had

once again asked it of him. The cat was long gone, leaving Reuben no friendly face to come home to.

All he wanted was another chance with Gladys. Not only did Reuben find her genuinely intriguing, he had also never before experienced being brushed off like a bothersome fly. Was he losing his touch? Getting too old?

Worse, what if she wasn't interested in him because she actually *saw* him for who he was… and there just wasn't enough substance for a woman of any intellect to be interested in? What if there was nothing he could do, nothing he could say, to earn a second glance?

Reuben pushed these thoughts out of his head as firmly as he could. Whether they were based on truth or not, such ruminations were counterproductive. What he needed to do was fortify the hard exterior of his rakish heart, then turn up his irresistible roguish charm to prove he still had some.

But how was he supposed to be charming and irresistible when he couldn't even find the object of his desire?

By the time his growling stomach indicated he'd missed luncheon, Reuben was practically despondent. His exhaustive search of the entire town of Marrywell had produced exactly no signs of Gladys. He wasn't ready to give up, but he didn't know which hotel she'd chosen to stay in, so there wasn't anywhere else left to search.

Besides, after six hours of unending disappointment at every turn, Reuben's current mood was unlikely to be irresistible or charming. He needed food, and he needed something to lift his spirits.

A new book would do. He'd finished the prior one last night, and was in need of a replacement. After consuming a hot cross bun from the bakery, he headed to the Blushing Maid Inn's familiar lending library. If there was to be no hope of finding Gladys, much less sharing a meal with her, at least he'd have a book to keep him company for an hour.

He strode through the lending library's open doorway, then came to an immediate stop.

Gladys was *right there*. Browsing a wall of books, one finger lightly tracing their spines, her back toward the doorway—and Reuben.

He'd recognize that attractive derrière anywhere.

He sauntered up to her and leaned a shoulder against the shelf she was perusing.

Her finger dropped from the spines. She turned toward him, her eyes widening in surprise.

Yet she was not nearly as surprised as Reuben was.

"Are you staying in this same hotel?" he blurted out, with a complete lack of casual rakish nonchalance.

She arched her brows and placed a finger to her lips. "*Shh.* This is a library. People are reading."

He cast a chagrined glance around the cozy room—only to realize it was utterly empty. Even the proprietor was off in the storage room behind the counter.

"*No one* is in here reading," Reuben said dryly.

Gladys removed a book from the shelves, opened it to a random place, and pointedly directed her full attention to the words on the page rather than the rake in the room.

Ouch.

Very well, then. Reuben would give her the space and the silence she desired.

He crossed to the counter to ring for the proprietor. Not only did Reuben already possess a subscription to this library, he had a book on order. It took the proprietor no time at all to find the promised tome on the influence of ancient Greece on modern roads and societal structure.

When Reuben turned back around, Gladys was no longer along the far wall. She had not fled from the room, however. She was over in the seating area, perched on a sofa cushion on the edge closest to the glow from the fireplace.

Despite the many open seats and tables, Reuben sat on the opposite end of the same sofa, in arm's reach of Gladys. Not that he reached for her, despite wanting to very much. With heroic effort, he didn't even look in her direction. He simply opened the book on his lap, turned to page one, and made his best attempt at actually reading the text therein.

Keeping his eyes on his page was the hardest thing he'd ever done.

Try as he might, his focus was drawn inexorably back to Gladys. She looked effortlessly beautiful and wickedly clever as her gaze flew over each sentence of the novel in her hands.

He wished he'd known she would be in here, so that he might have freshened up and maybe even dreamt up a book to read that would be more likely to impress her than his usual dry old tome on topics that only Reuben found fascinating.

Whatever salacious gothic drama Gladys was reading was the opposite of dry and boring. Occasionally her eyes would widen or her lips would twitch, and more than once, she grabbed the book tighter as though she herself risked being carried away with the action.

Reuben had never known how erotic it would be to watch a woman read.

Of course, the more he watched her from the corner of his eye, the less he wanted her attention on that book. He wanted to kiss her, to taste her. He wanted to feel her hands on his—

She glanced at him sharply.

He jerked his gaze back to his own volume and made a show of being fully absorbed in the text. What was he reading? Good God, still the table of contents.

"Enthralling stuff?" she said dryly.

"Hmm?" he said without looking in her direction, willing himself to appear as though nothing more than a studious reader absolutely riveted by... whatever words the letters on this page were meant to form.

As soon as Gladys returned her attention to her own novel, Reuben smoothed his lapels and ran a quick hand over his no doubt flyaway hair.

She lifted her gaze from her book again. He froze in place, hand on head, elbow jutting into the air.

Rather than glance toward him, she looked over at the clock in the corner.

Quickly, he arranged himself back into his nothing-to-see-here, just-a-man-enjoying-a-good-book pose.

Gladys closed her novel.

Reuben acted as though he hadn't noticed.

She rose to her feet and tousled his freshly smoothed hair. "You can stop pretending now. I'm leaving."

He glared up at her in consternation. In part because petting his hair felt so belittling, as though he were no more than a lap dog. Yet he longed for her to do it again. Wanted to feel her fingers gripping his hair and neck as he surged within her.

Unperturbed, Gladys strolled to the counter and returned her book.

"Thank you, Miss Smith," said the proprietor. "With luck, the volume you've been waiting for will arrive next week."

"I'll be gone by then," she replied with regret. "I'll have to look for it when I return to London."

She headed for the door.

Reuben gave up on feigning interest in his book and hurried to intercept her before she could disappear all over again.

"Have tea with me," he said when he reached her side.

"Unfortunately, I'm busy," she said with perfect politeness.

"But you would, if you weren't busy?"

"No," she replied with devastating frankness.

"Why not?"

"Tea sounds boring." She gave a little shrug. "We've already done that."

"All right, something new, then. Explore the labyrinth with me tomorrow. I'll arrange that picnic and we can eat it in the folly in the middle."

She gave him an arch look. "Won't that upset your admirers?"

"I hope it upsets yours," he muttered.

She heard him. "Why?"

He stared at her without speaking. Why? Because he didn't want to share her. A ridiculous notion, since Reuben didn't *have* her to begin with. But there it was. Possessiveness. He didn't want her to move on to someone else before giving him a chance. The very thought made him crawl out of his skin with jealousy.

Truly, Reuben wouldn't ask for much. He wasn't angling for a lifetime, or even love. Just one night. A chance to show her a splendid time, and to get this absurd obsession out of his system.

He fell into step beside her. "Can I walk you to your room?"

"No."

"You don't want me to know where it is?" he guessed.

She lifted a shoulder. "That's not where I'm headed."

"So you wouldn't mind if I knew which room was yours?" he asked hopefully.

She sent him a look. "If you want to know, earn it."

"I'm trying to. Tell me how," he begged.

She snorted. "I thought rakes could read minds."

Yes, that was the conceit of a practiced rake, was it not? Fulfilling every desire before the maiden in question could even properly formulate the thought. Seducing with ease, as though following choreographed steps to an inevitable conclusion.

He hadn't the least idea what was going on inside Gladys's maddening head. But he knew what he *wished* she was thinking. And had no problem giving it to her. Giving it to them both.

He tossed his book down onto the polished wooden floor and pinned her against the papered wall of the empty corridor. Now that his hands were free, he used them to cup her face and to angle his own mouth over hers.

She ducked out of his embrace before their lips could make contact.

"Noon," she said, and blew him a kiss. "At the entrance to the labyrinth. Make it worth my while."

And she sauntered off without a backwards glance.

Reuben stared after her until her footsteps no longer echoed in the corridor, then he adjusted his trousers and scooped up his fallen book.

Tomorrow. Tomorrow he'd seduce her and forget her.

And he'd very much ensure the experience was worth her while.

CHAPTER 12

With a lacy parasol perched over one shoulder at a jaunty angle, Gladys strolled toward the botanical gardens with a practiced casualness she did not feel.

In the twenty-odd hours since she'd left Reuben gaping after her retreating form outside the lending library, her mind had replayed the moment he'd almost kissed her countless times.

Yes. That had been exactly what she'd wanted, damn him. She'd wanted him to try to kiss her specifically so she could deny him, just as she'd done. But she'd also wanted him to kiss her, because she wanted to kiss *him*, despite all logic.

He was a rogue and a rake and a scoundrel and a hedonist and any number of similar epithets. He'd ruined her without a second thought when she was too young to understand the dangerous waters she'd waded into, and he'd do it again with the same self-indulgent carelessness if she let him.

She wasn't supposed to *really* fall for him. Even if it was nothing more than undiluted animal lust, and nothing so mortifying as actual feelings. In her storied career as a professional mistress, dredging up actual desire for her clients was part of the job. Just like seducing Reuben Medford and breaking his black heart was supposed to be.

But there he was, up ahead, looking nothing at all like a dangerous bogeyman, and everything like a wide-eyed lad, eager to lay eyes on the object of his affection.

As soon as he caught a glimpse of Gladys, he brightened visibly. Reuben waved as though he were a spectator at a royal parade, and she the revered princess on display atop an ornate carriage. Anyone would think him a smitten swain, delighted into raptures at the sight of his beloved.

Gladys had certainly believed that tripe once.

She pretended to block the sun from her eyes in order to allow her gaze to run over him. He appeared in intolerably raffish good looks today, with his wide shoulders encased in dove gray superfine and a stunningly folded white cravat above a robin's-egg-blue waistcoat. The hand that wasn't currently waving clutched the promised wicker picnic basket.

He rushed to meet her rather than allow her to finish her stroll to the mouth of the labyrinth alone.

"Good afternoon," he said, although it was five minutes before noon, and he had clearly been standing there waiting in anticipation since God-only-knew-when. "You're looking especially beautiful today."

"You look… somewhat tolerable."

He grinned at her. "I look nice and I know it, just like you look nice and you know it. There's nothing wrong with that."

"Humph," was her only reply.

She expected him to waste no time in offering

her his free arm, but he stood there smiling at her, as if he'd been waiting in this very spot since the night before, so eager was he to break bread with her in a hot, crowded garden.

Of course, now that he *hadn't* proffered his arm, she was overcome with the desire to reach out and touch it. To run her fingers over the soft fabric of his well-tailored sleeve, and learn the contours of the hard muscle beneath. Gladys steadied her breath. She forced herself to look over his shoulder, as if bored already by their encounter.

His free hand floated forward. Not to place her hand on his elbow, but to briefly tangle his fingers with hers, as though they were lovers forced to furtively clasp hands instead of launch themselves into each other's arms the way they truly wished.

She hoped the rascal did not hear her sharp intake of breath or glimpse the heightened pulse fluttering at her throat.

At last, he held out his arm.

She paused for effect before taking it. "Are you certain you want my fingers to wrinkle your fine tailoring?"

"I'll rip off every stitch posthaste to serve as a cushion for lovemaking, if that's one of the choices," he answered without hesitation.

She glared at him sternly. "It is not."

"Then I accept mere wrinkles." His brown eyes twinkled merrily. "For now."

She arched her brows as they set out along the labyrinthine path. "You're that certain you'll succeed at seducing me?"

He lifted his own eyebrows right back. "Are you that certain I won't?"

Gladys did not reply. The question of who was seducing whom had quickly become moot. The matter was no longer *if*, but *when*. This time, she would not relinquish control or toss her future away so foolishly.

This was revenge, pure and simple.

Well... a little complicated. Because men like him were meant to make intimate conquests, she couldn't ruin him the same way he'd ruined her. But she could dangle something he wanted in front of him, and snatch it away before he could claim it as his. Her heart would not belong to him.

The Despicable Medford had always got everything he'd ever wanted without even trying for far too long. He didn't respect women like her. Didn't see them as human beings. Just as vessels to be used and discarded.

By seeking commensurate vengeance, Gladys was essentially performing a public service for womenkind everywhere. A broken heart would teach him to value the next female to cross his path.

She just had to remember it was all only a game, and she the one controlling the board. She could not risk getting tangled in her own web and have her heart trampled on a second time.

When they reached the center of the hedgerow labyrinth, the folly where they were supposed to take their picnic was already full of people. The disgruntled expression on Reuben's face was so comical, Gladys half expected him to rush at the revelers with a lance, like Don Quixote beating back the windmills.

Instead, he collected himself and made a what-can-you-do shrug, then set down the basket right there on a grassy knoll in plain view of the folly and the pond and the entire pedestrian clearing.

"Your admirers will see you doting your attention on me," she warned him as she closed her lacy parasol.

"And steam shall rise from your admirers' ears as their brains melt into puddles of jealousy," he responded.

Simple to say, less simple to live through. Gladys could not help but anticipate with a measure of glee Reuben's undisguisable discomfort at being the center of attention in this way. The rake who could not be bothered to ask his conquests' names, visibly courting a woman in front of all his peers and in spite of their inevitable gossip.

But Reuben's attention never once strayed to their surroundings. As he spread the blanket and helped her to take a seat in the center, his focus remained one hundred percent on Gladys. The curious onlookers were no distraction. It was as though the rest of the world did not exist for him at all. Only Gladys mattered, and their picnic.

Or at least, that's how a practiced rake would want his target to feel.

She pulled a smooth flat rock the size of her palm out of her reticule and placed it beside the blanket on the grass, then removed the dainty hourglass from her reticule and set it atop the rock. Grains of sand immediately began to spill forth into the empty lower half.

Reuben sent her a cynical look. "I only have an hour?"

She lifted her shoulder. "Change my mind."

He smiled. "I'll do my best."

Of course he would. This sham romantic encounter was what a rake *did*. If she went home with him tonight and shared his bed the way he clearly expected her to do when presented with a simple picnic, he'd be back here tomorrow with someone else, making the next conquest.

"Why me?" she asked softly.

It was the question that had been eating away at her ever since that first encounter all those years ago—and its echo earlier this week, on the very same bench. Was it truly nothing more than random happenstance? A woman being in the wrong place at the wrong time and finding herself in the clutches of a conscienceless scoundrel?

Or might it be something more?

Was it unforgivably naïve that a small part of her still hoped that when he'd looked at her, he saw *her*, and not just the next innocent mouth to add to his collection of stolen kisses?

He frowned, as if the question confused him. "Why *not* you?"

"Let us speak plainly. You did not come to the matchmaking festival to make a match."

"It's true, I'm a committed bachelor," he admitted freely, not that there had been any doubt on the matter. "Nothing that happens will alter that."

At least he acknowledged the truth to her face this time. When they did consummate this flirtation, there could be no crying on either side when they parted ways and returned to being strangers.

"Let me guess… Why tie yourself to one woman when you can sample them all?" she asked wryly.

He hesitated, then gave a roguish shrug. "Something like that."

She waited, but he offered no further explanation for his relentless philandering.

Well, what more had she expected? A simple, base desire to nestle his cock between as many legs as possible was not only what she'd always believed about him, but also what he'd always claimed and how he'd always behaved.

Yet something about his reaction to her question made her think there was more depth there. Something that he was not sharing.

"Might we change the topic?" he asked lightly. "I do not want to waste any more grains of sand talking about other women. They don't matter. This picnic, here, with you, is what matters."

And that was it, wasn't it? The obvious answer: whenever he was with whomever currently happened to be present, no other women mattered. Not the one he'd kissed that morning, or the one he'd tumbled the night before. Just the one sitting in front of him—for as long as she held his attention. The moment she was out of sight... well, there'd be another woman to take her place. And another, and another. Each would be the only woman that mattered. For a minute, an hour, a night.

Then the poor wretch would discover the following morning, to her horror and humiliation, that she'd never mattered one whit at all.

"What's in the basket?" Gladys asked, forcing herself back on script. She could not let her disgust at his single-mindedness impede her plans for revenge. "You did not ask me what I might like."

"I was forced to guess," he agreed. "I hope at least one thing in this basket will meet your approval."

He placed his hand atop the wicker, but hesitated before lifting the lid.

She frowned. Something was off. Reuben was not how she remembered, nor quite what she'd expected. Handsome and charming and audacious and all that, but perhaps not quite as cocksure as he tried to project.

Either that, or Gladys was finally getting under his skin.

He met her eyes, then flung back the lid of the basket and reached inside.

She could not help but lean forward in anticipation. Nothing would have prepared her for what he drew out from the basket's shadowed depths.

"Here." He shoved a book onto her lap. "It's for you."

She picked it up in wonder.

This wasn't just any book. This was the latest volume in the series she had been devouring. The novel the proprietor of the lending library had not been able to obtain. Gladys had visited every inn and every library in Marrywell in search of this very item, all to no avail.

"Where did you find this?" she demanded.

He gave a crooked smile. "London."

"*London?*"

"When you left the lending library, I went back in and asked what it was that the proprietor had been unable to procure for you. He wrote down the title and author. I hope I managed to find the right one."

"Oh, it's the right one, all right." She wanted to hug the coveted volume to her chest. She wanted to hug *him* to her chest. After years of receiving money and jewels from her clients, for the first time, a gentleman had actually given her a gift she really wanted. Something personal, that only she would appreciate. "You drove to London and back in one night? When did you sleep?"

"In the back of the carriage." He rubbed the nape of his neck as though it still pained him, and gave a sheepish smile. "As much as anyone can sleep in the back of a carriage."

She stared at him. If this audacious man thought for one second that inconveniencing himself of time, money, and comfort in a mad hunt to find and present her with the latest book by her favorite author was the key to a woman's heart... Damn, he was good.

And far more dangerous than anticipated.

CHAPTER 13

*R*euben hoped his carefully arranged expression projected his mask of roguish confidence, and not the stomach full of nervous butterflies he was currently trying to hide.

Was the book a misstep? Should he have gone with roses? Sweets? A gold-and-diamond tiara? No gift?

The hourglass was already a quarter empty, and he had no notion of whether he was moving in the right direction—or going anywhere at all.

Her gaze lifted to his.

"Thank you," she said softly, her face radiant. "I plan to start reading this very night. In fact, if you have other business you'd rather attend to…"

Relief coursed through him. From the moment the wild idea had occurred to him, Reuben hadn't been able to get it—or her—out of his head. Truth be told, the trip to and from London had passed in a blur.

He'd spent the outbound journey making a list of every bookseller and reading library he could think of, refusing to even consider the possibility of defeat. Reuben would have knocked on the publisher's door at three o'clock in the morning and dragged him to his printing press in his nightclothes if that was what it took to get Gladys her book.

The inbound journey had been worse than a child awaiting Christmas. With the book safely in his hands, Reuben's overactive mind imagined every possible way he might gift it to Gladys, and what her reaction would be... from the sweet to the salacious.

Sending him away so she could start reading right then and there hadn't made the list, but he could not stop grinning at her regardless. He'd made her *happy*. A new experience that he liked better than he would have guessed.

Until now, he'd only pleased a woman with his hands and his mouth and his body. That he'd put this blissful look on Gladys's face without even touching her was heady and confusing and a little bit addicting. Now that he'd achieved it once, he wanted to do so again and again.

She placed the book on the grass next to her parasol. "Is there food in that basket, or is it full of literary surprises?"

The picnic. Right.

With alacrity, he set about divvying up the plates and the utensils, and presented her with the next round of offerings: every rumored aphrodisiac he could get his hands on. Oysters, chocolate, strawberries, fat, succulent grapes...

Surprising him, she caught on without any need for explanation and burst out laughing at the less-than-subtle sensorial feast.

The sound of her laughter warmed him just as much as her smile upon sight of her new book.

Conflicting emotions crawled beneath his skin

as he served her a plateful of decadent delicacies. What exactly was he doing here? Seducing Gladys, or wooing her?

This was supposed to be simple and straightforward. He had never before bothered pursuing the same woman twice, and still didn't quite understand how his old habits had got turned on their heads. He was a rake. He indulged sexual relations, not serious relationships.

Yet here he was, in sight of half of Marrywell, picnicking with a woman he hadn't even successfully managed to steal a kiss from the day before. Giving her a novel, rather than a tumble in the grass. Laughing, as though they were old friends, not anonymous lovers.

He liked her, was the problem.

And instead of convincing her to tup him, what he wanted most was for her to like him, too. He wanted to see her smile and to hear her laugh. He wanted her to throw that godforsaken hourglass into the nearby pond and never mention a time limit again.

Terrifying thoughts, for a man who was always the one to walk away.

But he was far from done with Gladys. For the first time in his life, Reuben wanted to take things slow. To come to know the woman herself, not just her body. He wanted her to wish to know him just as deeply.

This was baffling new territory, and he didn't have the least idea how to behave accordingly. He feared saying or doing the wrong thing, and losing her interest in every possible way before he learned the trick of this new game.

Reuben fully intended to win.

"Where in London do you live?" he asked as they dined.

She slanted him an unreadable look. "Not in Mayfair. I presume you do?"

"I do," he admitted. "It's…"

"Exclusive? Expensive? Unwelcoming to outsiders?"

"Probably all of that. I also spend a great portion of the year in Brighton. Do you visit the sea?"

"Sometimes. I prefer Bath. Delicious buns."

He grinned. "I like baths. And shapely buns."

She threw a grape at him. "You would."

"Don't you?" He popped the grape into his mouth.

"Doesn't everyone?"

He considered her. "I suppose you have a subscription to a lending library in Bath as well as London?"

"I do," she agreed. "I presume you have one in Brighton?"

"At Margate. There's a dedicated section for novels as well as for histories. You'd like it."

"Hm." She fluttered her lashes at him. "Something tells me I wouldn't be able to read a single word without a certain rake interrupting."

"I was reading my own book," he protested.

"It was upside-down."

"It was not! Was it?"

She laughed and shook her head. "You're dreadful at acting."

"I prefer to say things plainly," he admitted. "Fewer complications that way."

This was usually true, and the reason why Reuben's hummingbird-like inconstancy was the stuff of legend. He saw no reason to hide his nature or to pretend to want something he did not.

It was best to attract only like-minded individuals.

Of course, that was before he'd met Gladys. He had no idea what he was doing now, and couldn't speak plainly about his feelings on the matter if there was a dueling pistol to his head. He didn't usually *have* feelings when it came to these things. At least, nothing more profound than the enjoyment one got from a pleasant afternoon at the racetrack, or a good meal at one's club. A few hours of mindless indulgence and entertainment, nothing more.

But Gladys made him *think*. She made him *try*. He was twisted up in all manner of knots without the least notion how to make a straight line between the two of them.

It should be maddening. It *was* maddening. But somehow... not off-putting. He liked the challenge. He liked *her*. And it was quickly becoming evident that a few hours of mindless indulgence with her would not be nearly enough.

Especially the mindless part. Much the opposite. His brain would not cease cataloguing every detail about her. The location of her five freckles, the curl of her dark eyelashes, the rise and fall of her shapely bosom as she drew breath. Everything fascinated and bewitched him. He would not have got any more sleep had he remained in bed last night. His thoughts would have been plagued with images of Gladys either way.

"Do you think," he began, "that later we might—"

But she was already rising to her feet.

"What is it?" he asked, startled. "Has something happened?"

She lifted up the hourglass. "Time has run out."

It was a bittersweet victory to note that he'd at least managed to keep her attention for the entire hour this time.

"Tomorrow," he said quickly. "We can meet at the same time and place—"

"No more picnics. We've done that." She scooped up her book and her parasol.

Reuben racked his brain to think of what else he could offer her in this tiny, marriage-minded town.

"The brewer's field!" he blurted out. "There's ales to sample, and…"

And this was an activity one engaged in with one's equally dissolute gentlemen friends, not the Town lady one was trying to impress.

To his surprise, Gladys looked intrigued. "I do like a good ale. Hmm. All right, two o'clock. We can meet in front of the Blushing Maid Inn."

"We'll have another hour together?"

"Up to an hour." She wiggled the hourglass. "We'll see how it goes."

"I suppose we will." He smiled.

This time, he would make sure she had no interest in walking away.

CHAPTER 14

The following, slightly overcast afternoon, Gladys curled her hand around Reuben's elbow. Like yesterday, she would not be able to begin the countdown until they were settled at their final destination and there was somewhere stable to set her hourglass.

She wondered if he, too, realized he'd be allowed slightly more than his allotted hour, and if so, what he made of the development. Did he think he was winning? What game did he believe afoot?

When they'd first been reunited in the statue garden, she'd clearly meant no more to him than she had during their first disastrous encounter: a nameless, forgettable wench with which to exchange a torrid kiss—or more—and never think of again.

But the brewer's field they were quickly drawing closer to was not a place for seduction. It was crowded, hectic, and highly public. Much like the wide pedestrian area at the center of the hedgerow labyrinth.

If anyone was winning this game, it was Gladys. The rake was firmly on her hook, dangling helplessly in response to her every whim. That her deepest desire was revenge, not conjugal bliss, was a little secret he would discover soon enough.

Reuben grinned at her. "The brewer's field is just ahead."

"I had no idea," Gladys replied with a straight face.

The brewer's field could be heard long before it could be seen. When their steps drew them within a hundred yards, the dull roar of drunken conversations punctuated by the occasional clink of ale mugs drifted with the wind, despite the six-foot-tall boundary of thick, flowering elderberry bushes enclosing the eponymous field.

They entered through an open brass gate and were immediately greeted with a sea of scarred circular, gray stone tables, around which hundreds of happy men perched on old curved stone benches, drinking and speaking animatedly with their compatriots.

Gladys wasn't the *only* woman present... but it was close. This must be where the menfolk came whilst their wives and daughters were off shopping or promenading or taking tea in proper parlors like civilized ladies.

Gladys much preferred being uncivilized. She hadn't been proper in years. But she wasn't quite certain how to take Reuben's easy acceptance of her complicit behavior. Had he sussed her out as no sort of lady from the moment he'd grabbed her in the statue garden? Or was he so used to being around a fast crowd in London, that the idea of propriety was the farthest consideration from his mind?

"Any specific ale you'd like to try first?" he asked.

"I'll have what you're having."

"Then let's start here." He paused before the first vendor's booth and exchanged a coin for a pair of foaming ales.

Gladys accepted her half-pint with both hands.

"If the mugs are smaller than you're used to," he explained, "it's because these are meant to be samples. Brewers come from all over England to put up booths here during the festival, in the hopes of attracting new customers year round."

"It looks like it's working."

"Does it?" Reuben made a doubtful face. "Many of these men are so sotted, they wouldn't know a brewer from a badger if one bit them on the nose. The vendors hand out calling cards to anyone who asks, but after the fourth or fifth ale, I'd be surprised if anyone could remember the nuances differentiating their first mug from the second."

"At least the vendors are making money?"

"Good money, I imagine. Several of them have told me they raise more here in one week than they usually earn in an entire month."

"A frequent customer then, are you?"

"The frequentest." He grinned at her, and held out his mug. "To not remembering what this tastes like an hour from now."

She laughed and clinked her mug against his. They took their first sips at the same time, and ended up with matching froth mustaches, which they wiped away with the backs of their free hands.

"Shall we take a seat?" he asked.

"If there is one."

"Oh, there's always something. We might just have to venture a little further from the vendors to find a free table."

True to his word, Reuben discovered an empty

stone table nestled in a fragrant green corner where two elderberry hedgerows met.

Gladys settled herself on one of the squat, curved stone benches. Reuben took the seat next to her, rather than the bench opposite.

"Well?" he asked. "Are you picking up notes of oak and caramel and desperation?"

"Did you even taste yours?" she replied with a lift of her brows. "The primary flavor is toasted barley, balancing out the malt. The slight bitterness in the aftertaste is the perfect touch to round out this particular blend of roasted grains and fermentation."

He blinked in astonishment. "You *do* like ale!"

"I told you so, didn't I?"

"You didn't tell me you'd be the only person here who really would be able to distinguish nuance several pints later."

"We'll see how it goes," she said with a small half-smile. "This is only my first mug."

"I've no doubt you can do whatever you set your mind to," he said with confidence. "I should cease being surprised that you keep impressing me more with each passing day."

Cheeks flushing, she took a drink rather than respond. She reminded herself to stick to the plan. This was not courtship, but vengeance. The only way to regain a small piece of the autonomy, power, and dreams he had stolen from her.

Enacting her well-deserved revenge was turning out to be much harder than expected. Oh, not Reuben's part. He was even easier to ensnare than she'd dared to hope. The problem was Gladys. And the fact that the more time she spent with her sworn enemy, the less she hated him.

Belatedly, she recalled her hourglass and quickly placed it at the center of the stone table.

"I had dared to hope you'd forgotten," he said ruefully.

She almost had. Such was the danger of his company. The hourglass was meant to worm inside his head, and now served just as much for her sake. It was becoming increasingly evident that she could only resist him in short doses. An unchecked hour from now, she would still be able to distinguish notes of barley from malt, but might no longer remember the reason she was supposed to hate this handsome scoundrel with every ounce of her soul.

They finished their ale samples at the same time.

"Shall I retrieve the next round?" Reuben asked.

Gladys leapt to her feet. "My treat. Will you guard the table?"

"With my life." He gave a cheeky salute.

She wasn't supposed to care about his life, the same way he hadn't cared about hers. But as she hurried away from him to wander amongst the vendor booths, her feelings were very much in conflict.

On the one hand, he was exactly as she remembered. A spoilt, pleasure-seeking libertine with nothing but time on his hands and predictable selfish desires to indulge.

On the other hand, he was so much more than that. He was surprisingly studious and surprisingly clever and surprisingly thoughtful and surprisingly sweet and surprisingly... not all that bad, if one wasn't hoping to marry him.

And since Gladys most emphatically did *not* wish for a connubial future with Reuben or any

man, if they had met under any other circumstances, they might have wound up right here
where they were today, toasting each other with
glasses of ale without the least thought of old hurts
and fresh revenge.

All because the damnable man wasn't seducing
her or even courting her. His methods were far
more devastating: he was becoming her friend.

She purchased a pair of ales and made her way
back to the table as slowly as possible, in the hopes
that the hourglass would run out in her absence.

The sand had barely fallen at all. Either the rake
had been up to tricks whilst she was gone, or time
simply stood still when spent with him, despite the
sensation that every minute rushed by breathtakingly fast.

"What did you choose?" he asked with interest.

"I settled on a selection of…" She launched into
an unnecessarily detailed explanation, hoping to
bore him out of the look of disconcerting admira-
tion currently on his face.

No such luck. With each word, he seemed to
find her even more fascinating than before.

"I wish I could take you with me everywhere I
go drinking," he lamented with feeling. "Such expe-
riences would be infinitely better in your
company."

Damn him, how was she supposed to guard her
heart against comments like *that*?

This was what she wanted, she reminded herself. This was the plan, working. He was *supposed* to
fall in love with her, so that it would hurt all the
more when she discarded him, as he had done
to her.

But now, a dreadful little part of her wanted
him to fall head over heels not to exact revenge,

but because he finally saw her as a human worthy of love. Specifically, *his* love.

God only knew a shameful piece of her heart still held a foolish tendre for him.

"Why did you come to the matchmaking festival, if you weren't looking to make a match?" she blurted out.

"My uncle commanded my presence, and I was hoping for another glimpse of…" He dropped his gaze and glanced away. "Nothing. I was chasing a ghost. Boyish folly." His bright gaze flew back to hers and he smiled. "I much prefer finding you to the old dreams I left behind."

She made a rude sound with her lips. "Don't fling your rakish lines at me."

"I have to try," he protested. "What if they worked?"

She rolled her eyes and took a sip of her ale. "I don't even want to know how often it does work."

"None of my lines appear to work on you, so I've given up trying."

"Then what do you call the nonsense you just spouted?"

"The truth." His eyes held hers, his face serious. "I've had more fun in these stolen hours with you than all my prior days in Marrywell combined."

The same was true for her, though she would not voluntarily admit it.

"What about you?" he asked. "Are you here to make a match?"

"No. I came to settle a score."

"Ooh, intriguing. Is the score now settled to your satisfaction?"

"It's a work in progress."

"Isn't everything?" he said in commiseration, and tapped his mug to hers. "To your success."

She stared at him. If he had any idea what he'd just wished for...

"Did you start your novel last night?" he asked suddenly.

"Started and finished it," she admitted. "I was up almost until dawn."

"It was worth it?"

"Every sleepless minute."

He looked pleased. "I wish I felt half as passionately about my dusty old history tomes."

"I suspect you do," she said wryly. "It's just not very rakish to say so."

"All right, you've caught me. I can quote to you from many of my books. Do you know the difference between Hoplitai and Psiloi warriors?"

"Please don't tell me. Ignorance is bliss."

He harrumphed in faux petulance. "What was your book about, then?"

"You'd probably find it as stimulating as I find ancient warfare."

"I find *you* stimulating. What do you do when you're not reading?"

She took another sip to buy herself some time. Thus far, Gladys hadn't lied to Reuben about anything, though she'd refrained from volunteering a few choice details. What did she do when not reading?

This did not seem the environment in which to pronounce, *I engage in bedsport for money.* Or to proclaim that she was no longer welcoming men who took their pleasure without considering hers, and therefore intended to retire with her cat and her fireplace and many more books like the one she'd read last night.

"I was a hostess of sorts," she said at last. "But

I've tired of entertaining others. I cherish my moments of solitude."

"To read novels and skip rocks and drink yourself into oblivion?"

"That sounds like as good an afternoon as any."

"I don't know what it says about me that I agree with you." He gave a self-deprecating smile. "Rakes are also supposed to be born entertainers, but such exploits are boring more often than not. I enjoy a good book and I enjoy a good ale, though I admit I prefer playing cards with friends over skipping rocks."

"I enjoy playing cards," she admitted.

"Do you? What are your favorite games?"

"It's difficult to say. I rarely have an opportunity to join a game with others. Men have their gentlemen's clubs, but women... Mostly, I play solitaire."

"Most card games do require four or more players, but not all. Do you know Casino? It can be played with two."

"I know Casino." Gladys used to play it with her sister, before she'd been ruined and banished.

He leaned forward, ale forgotten. "Come to my room, tomorrow. We'll play all the Casino you can stand. I'll provide the ale."

She narrowed her eyes. "Why do I feel like I'd be walking into a spiderweb?"

"Because you're an astoundingly suspicious shrew," he said cheerfully. "And because if I can manage to steal a kiss between the card-playing, I absolutely will."

"What makes you think I want a kiss?"

"What makes you think you won't?"

Nothing made her think that. She did want a kiss. Was burning for a kiss. Ducking out of his embrace every time he reached for her was the hardest thing she'd had to do in years.

The next time he kissed her would be even worse. Unlike the first few encounters, this time, he would mean it. He'd be reaching for Gladys, not some nameless stranger in a garden. He'd be kissing the woman he picnicked with, and played cards with, and drove to London and back in the dead of night to buy a gothic novel for.

And Gladys wouldn't be faking her desire either, blast him. She'd laid a trap for the Despicable Medford and stepped into its sharp jaws herself.

She glanced at the hourglass on the table. Empty. How long had it been empty?

She snatched it up like King Arthur brandishing his sword and scrambled to her feet. "I must go."

Reuben rose as well, his warm brown eyes locked on hers. "Tomorrow? My room?"

It was a wonderful idea. A terrible idea. The perfect opportunity to put the final step of her plan into motion.

"Tomorrow," she managed. "Four o'clock."

His smile was brighter than the sun. "I'll be waiting."

Waiting, then soon after, he'd be weeping. Because when Gladys was through with him, she would walk away without looking back, and wipe him from her mind altogether, the same way he'd done to her. Reuben wouldn't become a memory. He'd be nothing at all. By this time next week, she'd be safe and sound back home, and have forgotten him entirely.

She hoped.

CHAPTER 15

*R*euben spent the entirety of the following morning preparing his rooms for Gladys's arrival.

First came artful decorating with candles. A vase of fresh flowers here, a vase of fresh flowers there. Then he got rid of the excess candles, because they were too much. Then the flowers looked like too much, so he got rid of those, too. Then it wasn't enough, and he was forced to buy more flowers and prepare a few candles after all.

The problem wasn't the room. The problem was Reuben. Beneath his rakish veneer, he was nothing more than an idle, lonely bookworm, whose idea of scintillating conversation was to blurt out aspects of Greek historical influence before he'd even imbibed his ale. Of course an intelligent woman like Gladys would run away from the real him.

He would pretend to be whatever it took for her to give him a few more precious moments of her time. If only he knew what that *was*.

By the time she finally knocked on his door, Reuben was no longer sure his shoes were even on the right feet. After sending away his valet for privacy, Reuben had immediately repented. In the past hour, he'd dressed and undressed and re-dressed twelvefold, redoing his cravat and his coiffure every time. He and his rented rooms were as clean and presentable as possible, giving an air somewhere between *Don't worry, this is definitely not a seduction* and *But of course it can become one in an instant, if a seduction is what you want.*

"Good afternoon," he said breathlessly as he answered the door.

The breathlessness was not because he'd sprinted at top speed across the room the very second her knuckles touched the wood door panel, although that was exactly what he had done.

The breathlessness was because he always forgot to breathe whenever he looked at her.

Gladys did not have the least air of frantic costumery. She looked calm and collected and utterly captivating in a simple gown of pale rose sprigged muslin, with her hair gathered behind her head and only a single brown tendril framing half of her captivating face.

One of her dark eyebrows lifted with amusement. "And a fine afternoon to you, good sir. Am I interrupting something?"

"What? No, I... Come in, come in." He stepped aside and welcomed her into the small parlor.

After much deliberation, he'd left the door to his bedchamber shut tight. Closing it off made the available space seem even smaller, but at least for the moment, the look he was going for was *cozy*, not *mouth of the dragon*.

He motioned her over to the sofa, armchairs and tea table, upon which latter object stood a covered dish, two place settings, and a pair of crystal wine glasses.

"Wine?" she asked. "I thought you promised ale."

"I have ale if you want it," he said quickly, "but I fear toasted barley won't go as well with fresh pudding as an inch or two of fine port."

She took her seat, and set her infernal hourglass atop the table. "I do like port. And pudding. Where did you get it?"

"From the very best chef in the region," he assured her.

"The pudding competition?" she guessed. "Who won it this year?"

"I didn't catch her name," he admitted and started to take his seat.

An odd look flashed across Gladys's face.

He paused. "If you're not peckish, we can jump straight into cards?"

Her face smoothed. "I'd have to be dead not to have room for pudding."

Relieved, he reached for a serving spoon and scooped a portion of hot, crumbly pudding onto each of their plates. After pouring a bit of port into each crystal goblet, he lifted his glass toward hers. "To good wine, good food, and a good game."

She touched the lip of her glass to his, then sipped her port. "Mm, this is quite decadent."

"From my private collection," he confessed. "Some things, one cannot leave up to the cellar of one's inn."

She sent him a considering look. "Do you always travel with your private wine collection, or is this a special occasion?"

"I... *might* have picked out the best bottle I

could find during my jaunt back to London in search of your book."

Her lips twitched. "You did a fine job."

"Thank you." He picked up his fork. "Try your pudding."

She scooped some up obediently. When she placed it into her mouth, the euphoric look upon her face was reminiscent of rapturous expressions Reuben had only ever previously seen in bedchambers. Even her eyes fluttered closed in ecstasy.

"No wonder this won," she said in awe. "This pudding is better than opium."

"Are you an aficionado of opium as well as ale?"

"To be honest, I've not tried any. All I hear is that opium is addicting. Like this fig pudding. Already I've given up all my hopes and dreams for the future, if I can spend every moment instead in the kitchen of whoever made this delicious pudding, sampling their every batch."

"I'll learn to make it," he said without thinking, then wished he hadn't. The look on Gladys's face was startled, to say the least.

He belatedly realized his comment could be interpreted as *please live the rest of your life in my house*. Practically tantamount to a marriage proposal. "I mean, I'll ask for the recipe. And share it with you."

"I'd appreciate that." Her expression was still guarded as she took another bite of pudding.

The problem was, for a brief moment, Reuben had meant his comment exactly how it had sounded. He wanted to put that look of ecstasy back on Gladys's face again and again, by any means possible. His longtime preference might have been via the bedroom, but if the same effect could be achieved with a hot pan of fig pudding, he wasn't above tying on an apron and learning how to cook for her this very afternoon.

As for the rest of the package… well. The reason he would not be proposing marriage wasn't because of any perceived lack on Gladys's part, but due to Reuben's fundamental unsuitability as a husband. Keeping his liaisons quick and casual was the kindest thing a man like him could do for a woman. Doing so ensured that she always reserved the option to walk away.

Which was no doubt what any halfway intelligent woman would choose to do, if she had the misfortune to get to know the real Reuben.

And Gladys was no fool.

CHAPTER 16

*I*f this was to be their last hour together, Reuben wanted it to be everything she wished.

Tonight was the festival's final grand ball. On the morrow, everyone would be returning to their homes. To his disappointment, this might be the last time he would ever see Gladys. Reuben didn't even know which room was hers in this hotel, much less have any idea how to find her in London —a city of one and a half million people.

For now, he picked up the cards and dealt her in. "You know the game?"

"I know the game." Her expression was oddly melancholy. Almost wistful.

"Is there something you'd rather play than Casino?" he asked carefully.

"Casino is fine." She visibly shook off her strange doldrums and flashed him a suspiciously bright smile. "I was just remembering when I used to play every night with my sister. But those days are long gone."

Reuben's fingers faltered as he dealt the cards. The way Gladys had phrased that sounded so final.

Had something happened to her sister? He was curious, but didn't want to pry. He settled on letting her know that family was a welcome topic, if it was one she wished to pursue.

He straightened the deck of cards. "Do you come from a large family?"

"No." She glanced at the four cards face up on the table. "Just my parents, my sister, and me. What about you?"

"No siblings, I'm afraid."

"The sole child." She peeked at her cards. "Spoiled rotten since birth, I presume?"

"I wouldn't have it any other way."

Except it hadn't been that way for long. His parents had died when Reuben was young, and he'd gone to live with an uncle who had no time or interest in acknowledging a brokenhearted little boy. As he grew and discovered he could attract attention another way—by becoming a rake—he had thrown himself wholeheartedly into the endeavor and never looked back.

Until now.

Nonetheless, he made a wide-eyed, faux innocent rake face. "I wouldn't know what to do if I weren't on everyone's tongue."

Gladys snorted. This time, the slight smile at the edges of her lips appeared genuine. "I imagine you wouldn't. I didn't come from money, but my parents spoilt my sister and me as best they could with attention and love. Their hope was that their daughters would each make a fabulous match, to a man of wealth and standing—and, obviously, impeccable taste in women."

He had no doubt Gladys could make such a match before the sand ran out on her hourglass.

And yet, she remained unwed. "You had no interest in marriage?"

"I longed for it," she said softly. "Nothing sounded more romantic than being swept off my feet by a man in love."

He frowned. "You didn't like any of your offers?"

"There weren't any legitimate ones." She scooped up the three of hearts and the four of clubs with the seven of diamonds. "What about you? How many offers have you made?"

"None. But I suspect you knew that."

"That *is* what the gossips say. But they also say you are never seen more than once in the company of the same woman."

And here he was, spending time with her. As he had done every day of the festival since his arrival, both publicly and privately.

He matched his king to the one on the table. "Perhaps people change."

Gladys's eyes flew to his, her surprisingly serious gaze piercing. "Do they?"

"Have you never changed?"

"Oh, I've changed." She laughed lightly. "I think it's safe to say you wouldn't recognize me as the naïve debutante I once was. Have you not always been a glutton, flitting from flower to flower like an insatiable honeybee?"

"Not the most flattering depiction of my personality, but an apt one. Yes, I have always been a rakehell."

"*Is* 'rakehell' a personality?" she asked skeptically.

"What else would it be? A divine calling?"

"A symptom."

He snorted and dealt the next round. "Is pleasure-seeking a disease?"

"No," she said without hesitation. "Sometimes it is a necessity. The best way to relieve suffering is with pleasure."

"You think I suffer?" he asked in surprise. "I'm rich, well-connected, handsome…"

"And breathtakingly humble," she teased as she arranged the cards in her hand. "Yet many people who seek pleasure in the arms of strangers suffer from loneliness."

"I'm not lonely," he protested.

She scooped up two fives with a ten. "Aren't you? Reuben Medford, the most prolific rake in all of England, spending the final day of the largest local festival indoors, playing a game of cards."

"Maybe I *like* cards."

"When not walking alone through an empty woods, or sitting in solitude with yet another dense tome on ancient history."

He stacked a pair of sevens. "All that means is that I exercise my brain as well as my body."

"Who also is available at the drop of a hat to accompany an aging spinster to labyrinths and brewer's fields and lending libraries and picnics. Or to dash off to London in search of a gothic novel you have no interest in reading."

"Maybe I like…" Aging spinsters? That wasn't the common denominator at all—or a fair description. He lowered his cards and held her gaze. "Maybe I like *you*."

She arched her brows. "I'm to believe you canceled your scheduled plans and cleared your busy days *and* nights on the off chance of spending an hour with me?"

That was exactly what Reuben had done,

though he had not realized the enormity of it until hearing his actions phrased in this manner.

"You were free, too," he shot back in defense, though this was a weak sally.

The truth was, he had spent a good portion of the past days unsuccessfully searching for Gladys, which would imply that *she* was off being actually busy somewhere, whilst he was merely busy thinking about her.

"I had an hour to spare," she agreed, and matched a pair of eights.

Disgruntled, he dealt the next round with dramatic flair.

Unperturbed, she picked up her new cards and added them to her hand. "Have you been back to the river to practice skipping stones?"

"Yes," he admitted. Celebrated rake, choosing to be all alone in a forest, just as she'd said. "I've improved substantially, though I'm sure I could use another lesson."

"I'm happy to teach you a lesson," she murmured, and played her next card. "I hope you learn it this time."

Reuben frowned. "He of the dense tomes, remember? This old dog is capable of new tricks."

"Then don't you want something else from your life? Or do you imagine yourself forty years from now, a lecherous old roué, hobbling about ballrooms with a cane and a quizzing glass, squinting lustfully after the newest crop of blushing misses in pastel gowns?"

That did not sound flattering… *or* fulfilling.

"First of all," he informed her, "Forty years from now, fashions will have changed, and young misses might no longer be decked in insipid pastels."

"Very true." She matched a trio of twos. "I stand corrected."

"Secondly, I shall not at that future time, nor do I now, angle after debutantes of any flavor."

She met his eyes. "Have you never?"

Instantly, his mind flooded with memories of a night long ago, when he'd grabbed the wrong woman in a statue garden and wondered if she'd been the right one after all. But of course she hadn't. Less than an hour after kissing Reuben, he'd learned Alsop had already claimed her. No matter how hard Reuben tried to forget her, the news that Alsop had wed made the rounds less than a month later.

At least Reuben had managed to avoid running into the happy couple in the years since.

But all he said aloud was, "I have done my best to make my dishonorable intentions clear, and to keep the company of those whose interest in passing pleasures aligns with my own."

"That is what they say," she agreed, and played her next card. "Don't you tire of being gossiped about?"

He shrugged. "The gossips do half of my work for me. The marriageable young misses know to stay away, and the adventuresome lasses with no reputation to mind know just where to find me."

Gladys nodded. "At home. Reading a book."

"You like to read, too," he pointed out.

"I *love* to read. I'm not ashamed of it in the least. I intend to spend the rest of my life reading as many lurid novels as humanly possible."

"That's not lonely?"

"I'm never alone. I inhabit the same worlds as the characters. Also I have a cat. Count Whiskers is never far from my lap."

Reuben could just imagine. "Where is Count Whiskers now? In your room?"

"In London," she said with a sigh. "He doesn't travel well, so I was forced to leave him at home. A friend is taking care of him."

A frisson of jealousy rippled through him. "A female friend?"

Gladys arched her brows. "No. Is there a question you'd like to ask me?"

"Yes," he blurted out. "Are you romantically involved with someone else?"

"Else?" she repeated drolly. "No, I'm not involved with anyone romantically."

Well, he'd deserved *that*, hadn't he? After all his insisting that he was a gluttonous rake with the attention of a gnat and no interest in marriage, he could hardly blame her for not finding his attentions particularly romantic.

And yet, what other explanation did he have for his behavior this past week? Every thought had been of her, every action calculated to find her, to please her, to care for her.

But how was she supposed to know all that, if he didn't tell her?

"I…" he began, and hesitated.

Tell her what, exactly? Was that not the question she was asking him? What his intentions were toward her, if not purely carnal?

"I'd like to meet Captain Whiskers," he managed.

"*Count* Whiskers," she corrected him. "He's Italian aristocracy, and he far outranks you. I'll let you know what he decides."

Reuben's spirits rose. Yes, to be sure, Gladys had meant that comment as a set down, but *I'll let you know* implied the two of them would meet again in the future.

Oddly, his imagination did not immediately picture a sweaty tangle of limbs and bedsheets, but rather a cozy afternoon much like this one, with a crackling fire and a game of cards or a good book, and Count Whiskers purring between their feet.

He tried not to think too hard about what it meant that he could imagine quiet nights at home with her as easily as sensual encounters. Skipping rocks by the river, perhaps, with him stealing kisses between each throw. Picnicking in a secluded clearing, and christening the blanket afterwards. Reading on opposite ends of a couch, their feet in each other's laps, a bottle of wine awaiting them. Waking up in each other's arms and making love before a leisurely breakfast, followed by—

"You're making the oddest expression," she told him.

He collected himself. "I was thinking about kissing you."

"Remembering the last time, or plotting the next one?"

"Both, always." He put down his cards. "Would it shock you if I said I want nothing more in this world than to make love to you?"

"Nothing shocks me." She set down her cards as well. "As for lovemaking, I've spent the last five years as a courtesan. Have I shocked *you*?"

Shocked? Hardly. So many of her previous odd comments and unusual behaviors now made sense. Of course a courtesan would catch on to his aphrodisiac picnic, and not be accompanied by a chaperone.

He shook his head. "I should be in a far worse

pickle if you were a virgin. If anything, I'm relieved. And jealous."

"Jealous of my past lovers?"

"Jealous of your superior cleverness. *I* should have been a cicisbeo for money. Ordinary rakes don't earn a single penny for their services, no matter how much in demand they find themselves." He wiggled his brows. "Unless you'd like to be my first paying customer?"

She laughed. "You wish I would."

"With every breath in my lungs," he agreed. "All right, you drive a hard bargain. First encounter, free of charge."

She tossed a pair of nines at him. "It's easy to jest when it's not your life. Becoming a courtesan wasn't my childhood dream. I was forced into it by circumstances outside of my control."

His hackles rose. "Forced how?"

"My final season out, a scoundrel ruined me so thoroughly, my family had no choice but to cut all ties with me to save my younger sister's reputation. I ended up on the street, surviving by any means necessary."

Anger flashed through Reuben, and his fists clenched in fury. "Of all the unconscionable... Someone should teach that blackguard a lesson!"

"On that, we agree," she murmured. "I'll never forgive him for losing me my family."

His heart clenched in sympathy. Choosing a life of solitude was one thing. Having one's loved ones snatched away was unforgivable.

"There's nothing wrong with sexual relations," he told her. "And there's nothing wrong with exchanging services of any sort for money. But neither situation should be forced upon you."

"Well, I'm finished with all that now. From this

month forward, I am no longer on the market. I shall select my lovers based on my desires, not theirs."

"Starting this very day?" he said with interest. "Because—you may not know this—there's a perfectly serviceable bed just on the other side of that closed door."

"How disappointing," she said with a little sigh. "A self-proclaimed rake who thinks lovemaking can only take place on a bed."

In a blink, he was on his feet and pulling her into his arms.

Reuben devoured Gladys with ravenous kisses, and she responded just as voraciously. Her hip bumped the table and the cards went flying. He swung her out of the way and against the wall, pinning her against the wood paneling. She sank her fingers into his hair and held on tight.

He kissed her as though his life depended on it. As though she was his entire world. He loved her taste, still sweet from the pudding. Her scent, so soft and feminine. The feel of her curves pressed lushly against him.

His heart beat faster than a hummingbird's wings, but it was all for her. Every pulse of his blood, every breath in his lungs, every heady second of not knowing which way was up because all directions pointed him right back to her.

He desperately hoped these were not the final moments they spent together, but the first hour of many, many more. He wanted these kisses every day and every night. Wanted to keep Gladys safe in his arms every waking second.

Reuben could not believe his good fortune in having her pressed up against him here and now. If he hadn't allowed himself a maudlin moment to get lost in the past, if he hadn't reached out and pulled her to him that night in the statue garden, he would never have known just what it was he'd truly been missing all these years.

He couldn't allow her to disappear from his life like that other young lady had long ago. Now that he'd found the person with which he could imagine himself passing blissful day after pleasurable night together, he could not possibly go back to how things were before. He had no interest in hunting ballrooms for prey. The only woman he wanted, the only person he needed, was right here in his arms.

He was suddenly, viciously glad Gladys was no longer a practicing courtesan. He held no rancor toward her past clients, but he could not bear the thought of the woman he loved forgetting all about him and opening her arms to—

Oh, shite. *The woman he loved.*

He held her closer. One night would never be long enough. What he really wanted was forever.

CHAPTER 17

*G*ladys knew better than to allow herself to believe there were real feelings driving this blaze of passion, but her damnable heart surged in hope all the same.

For five long years, she had prided herself on her unwavering commitment never to develop feelings for any of her clients. It turned out, she could not have given her heart away if she'd tried: it already belonged to someone else.

Love was for fools, and she was the biggest fool of them all! She *knew* what Reuben was: a butterfly, a bee, a feckless, careless rake. He'd made no attempt to hide that his interest in her was physical. That every action was calculated to seduce, not to woo.

And yet, even knowing all this, he had managed to make her feel courted as well as seduced. She was kissing him with abandon not because it was the next step in an elaborately planned vengeance stratagem, but because she *wanted* to kiss him, burned to kiss him, was desperate for any part of him that he would let her have.

She still had enough wits about her to know

that whatever this was, it would not last beyond tonight. Reuben was infamous for not giving his past conquests a second look, and Gladys... Well, she was achieving several goals at once: scratching a half-decade-long itch to finish what they'd started in that garden all those years ago, and showing Reuben just what he'd been missing. What he would *keep* missing, once she rolled out of bed and strolled off without so much as a fare-thee-well.

"Bed" being a figurative term, in this case. The way things were going, he was just as likely to take her here against this wall as to bother searching out a horizontal surface.

They were too busy kissing to waste time on conversation. Reuben seemed as inflamed and as desperate to have her as Gladys felt about him. His hands cradled her face, roamed her body, gripped her midsection, hauled her to him. His arousal was evident between them, hard and hot and insistent against her belly.

He swung her away from the wall and toward the sofa. Her skirts tangled with the tea table, sending the rest of the playing cards flying, and her trusty little hourglass tumbling to the floor.

There it was, then: no safety net. There would be no way to know when the hour was through. Walking away would be up to Gladys and whatever was left of her self-control... and self-respect.

Reuben laid her atop the sofa cushions with surprising gentleness, as if taking great care not to break this new toy before he'd had the opportunity to fully play with it.

Gladys knew what came next: up with the skirts, down with the trousers, then several dozen sweaty thrusts before a loud grunt, followed by a shuddering collapse into semi-consciousness.

She was right about exactly one of those things.

Her skirts came up, and Reuben's head went down. He knelt between her legs like a man at prayer, whose only wish was to worship what he found before him.

She gasped in shock and pleasure at the sensation of his tongue licking and swirling against her. She hadn't thought she could feel more desire for him than she already did, but with every intoxicating lick and swirl, her blood pumped faster and what was left of her brains evaporated altogether.

"Do you like it like this?" he murmured against her cleft between sensual licks.

Did she... like it like... *this*? She could barely think from pleasure, every limb simultaneously boneless and yet tensed in anticipation of the impending climax that teased ever so close to release.

No one had ever asked her if she *liked* what they were doing before. Her wishes weren't even an afterthought. They didn't signify. Her pleasure was as inconsequential as her opinions on the matter.

The fact that Reuben cared enough to ask was almost enough to push her over the edge.

"Y-yes," she stammered, when she found her breath. "I... like."

"Hmm," he purred against her trembling body. "Let's try to find something that you love. How about this?"

Without ceasing his tongue's expert seduction, he slid his hands up her thighs and pulsed a finger inside her.

She shattered at once, her thighs clutching his shoulders as she came apart against his face.

He did not stop until the tremors faded, then

made his way up her body, kissing her midsection, her bosom, her neck. He pulled her to him, limp as a rag doll, and chuckled softly against her ear.

"Might I unlace your gown, or are you too knackered to continue?"

Permission. All that, and he still sought permission to tup her. As if there was anything in this world that she wanted more.

"I suppose," she managed breathlessly, "I might be able to spare another minute or two."

He grinned as he flipped her atop him, cuddling her to his chest as he made short work of the ties binding the flaps of her gown together. In seconds, the soft muslin tumbled free from her shoulders. He hiked up her skirts, raising the gown and her shift together, up over her hips, her chest, her head. The garments fluttered to the floor beside the sofa with a soft whoosh.

He positioned her so that she was seated upright, her knees on either side of him. Without delay, he whipped off his dark gray dress coat, his blue silk waistcoat, his white cambric shirt. Now his upper body was as naked as hers was.

She ran her palms over the muscles of his arms, his shoulders, his chest. He coaxed her forward until her breasts dipped toward his waiting mouth. He licked and suckled. When she once again gasped for breath, he slid his hands from her breasts down toward her core and began to tease again with his fingers.

Her body quickened instantly, swirling her back up to the edge of the precipice. Before she tumbled anew, she fumbled for the fall of his trousers, releasing the stiff member that had been pulsing against her.

Once freed, she expected him to drive the action. Instead, he grasped her hips and placed her just over the tip, but did not surge upwards to penetrate her fully.

"You lead," he said, his voice strained and husky. "That way you can control the speed and the depth."

A sense of primal feminine power flooded her, and she sank onto his shaft without delay.

He moaned in relief, dark lashes fluttering as his eyes rolled back in pleasure.

She experimented with speed and depth and angle; sometimes slow and deliberate, sometimes fast and hard, sometimes shallow and teasing, sometimes so deep her mons ground sensuously against him. Each position brought even more pleasure than the last.

"Good God," he muttered, his passion-drunk eyes locked on hers. "I hope you're as close as I am. We have approximately thirty seconds before I explode."

Knowing *she* had done this to him was all it took for her body to give a little clench of delight. He let out a groan, as though willing himself not to let go yet, and placed his thumb just above where their bodies joined, teasing her back.

She came at once, her inner muscles spasming around him as he drove deep within her.

The moment she collapsed forward, sated, he yanked his shaft out from between her thighs, cradling her to his chest with one arm as the other swiped his handkerchief up off the floor and over his member. Reuben spent himself into its folds, hips jerking.

He tossed the soiled cloth aside and wrapped his arms about her, holding her close, as though she was even more precious to him now, than she'd been when their bodies had been joined.

His heart thundered against her ear, its galloping beat steadying slowly as his breath and hers returned to normal.

Nothing else was normal about this. Gladys had felt seen, desired, *cherished* in a way she had never before known—and was loath to lose again. She didn't want this to be the last moment in his arms. The very thought was enough to clog her throat with unshed tears.

Her quest for vengeance had brought her more pleasure than she had ever dreamt—and was also about to bring her unbearable pain.

Walking away from the man she loved might or might not wound Reuben...

But Gladys would be destroyed forever.

CHAPTER 18

*G*et up, Gladys scolded herself. *Get up and walk away.*

But how the devil was she supposed to pry herself out of the warm embrace of a man who was holding her to him as though she was the single most precious thing he had ever encountered?

Her gown and shift were still on the floor, next to the toppled hourglass. Nothing encased her bare limbs but a pair of silk stockings, tied above the knees with red ribbons. She should have been freezing. Instead, she was cozy and warm, nestled against the heat of Reuben's firm body like Count Whiskers nuzzling into her lap to be petted.

And he *was* petting her. One of his hands rubbed her back, less like a massage and more as if he was assuring himself she was really there and not a remnant of a dream. His other hand occasionally stroked her hair, one idle finger toying with the loose ringlets that had escaped from her long-destroyed chignon.

The sporadic gooseflesh that danced upon her skin had nothing to do with the temperature, and everything to do with her own disbelief that even after having finally achieved his wicked way with her, the ton's most infamous rake showed no signs of wishing her to be gone so that he could resume the hunt for his next conquest.

By all appearances, Reuben had no desire for her to leave his embrace, much less exit his rooms and his life. All of which made this the *perfect* time to do just that, striking when he least expected. Perhaps tossing a disparaging comment over her shoulder as she flounced out the door.

But Gladys could not currently flounce anywhere. She was too boneless, too sated, too *safe* and sound and snuggled. The low fire crackling in the grate wasn't half so lovely as the comforting warmth emanating from every inch of Reuben's body.

"I should go," she murmured.

"Should you?" His hands stilled, then began rubbing again. "Why don't you stay? Please. Stay the night, with me."

Please. Her breath caught. This was indeed the absolutely perfect time for a biting comment and a curt goodbye.

It would destroy him as surely as it would destroy her.

But her dress was so far away, there on the floor just out of reach. And her room was all the way up a flight of stairs and around a corner. And it was so very relaxing to have him stroke her hair and her back, whilst she listened to the calming beat of his heart.

Maybe she was wrong about him. Or maybe she had *been* right, once upon a time and for many years after, only for him to grow and change when she least expected it.

If he was not the scoundrel he was before, then she would not be exacting vengeance on the same man she'd spent all these years cursing for what he'd stolen from her.

She'd be spiting herself, for no reason at all.

"I don't know if that's wise," she said hesitantly. "The sand has long since run out of my hourglass, and we both know that you pride yourself on avoiding prolonged entanglements. Never twice with the same woman, isn't that right?"

His cheeks flushed with embarrassment. "That was the old me."

"Old as in… eight days ago?"

"Gladys, you cannot possibly think…" He framed her face with his hands, his eyes bright and earnest. "Don't tell me this week spent together didn't mean half as much to you as it did to me."

Tentative petals of hope, long forgotten, stirred in her belly. "I thought this was an extended seduction."

"I thought that, too… until the first moment we exchanged words, there by the folly. From then on, the more time I spent in your company, the more evident it became that my life would be the worse without you in it."

Her lungs utterly ceased being able to breathe. That was it. Gladys was going to suffocate to death right here, naked, atop a rake.

"I don't want you for one night," he continued, his intense gaze unwavering. "I want you every night. And every day. And every moment in between."

Suffocating and perished. Gladys was now extinct. The despicable, untrappable, coldhearted Reuben Medford was proposing marriage to a ghost. Her spirit had left her body.

He gave an abashed, lopsided smile. "Sorry if I'm doing this wrong. As you've pointed out, I haven't done this before."

"You're doing splendidly," she whispered. "I haven't done this before, either."

A frown wrinkled his brow, and he lowered his hands from her face. "I thought you said…"

The butterflies in her stomach turned into shards of glass, whipping against every corner with the force of a tempest. "You thought I said… what, exactly?"

"Didn't you tell me you'd spent the past several years as a courtesan? I presumed you'd meant you'd had several protectors over that time, but I guess they could've all been single encounters. What I'm trying to say, is that I cannot think of anyone else I'd rather have for my first mistress. You—"

Every muscle stiff with hurt and humiliation, Gladys picked herself up from Reuben's bare chest, dropped to the floor, and scooped up her fallen shift and gown.

Reuben blinked at her. "What are you doing?"

She pulled her shift on over her head, then did the same to her gown. It was awkward to tie the cord closed all by herself from this angle, but not as awkward as extricating herself posthaste from this horrible conversation.

"Is it the money? We haven't discussed a fee." He propped himself up on his elbows. "I'm rich, Gladys. You can name your price."

She considered kicking his shirt and coat into the fire. With regret, she settled on retrieving her fallen hourglass instead.

Reuben shot upright, alarm writ large all over his face. "You're not going, are you?"

Going and gone. Never to darken his door again.

She crossed the room in a handful of strides, her footfalls surprisingly steady despite the shaking of her legs and the nausea roiling in her stomach.

"Gladys, wait!" He leapt up from the sofa to sprint after her.

"Goodbye, Reuben." She opened the door. "I've heard—and had—enough."

With that, she stepped out of his life and closed the door firmly behind her.

CHAPTER 19

*R*euben froze in place, his face flaming with humiliation and his stomach turning over.

She didn't want *him*.

It was his worst fear, come nauseatingly, mortifyingly to life. That anyone who came to know the real man behind the rake wouldn't want anything further to do with him. It was the true reason he never had more than one encounter with the same person. A single tryst, with a minimum of conversation. That was how much of Reuben the average woman wished to have.

His body was attractive. His true self, less so. Well-honed skills made him an exceptional lover, which added to his mystique and infamy. But it still wasn't enough. The woman he loved was a courtesan who had lain with god only knew how many dullards, and even *she* didn't want a second go with Reuben. No matter how much money he offered.

The door closed behind her with sickening finality.

Not with a slam. A slam would imply passion.

Some degree of *caring* that she'd tied Reuben into knots and then sliced him in two.

Just a delicate, but firm *click*. No dramatics. No hesitation. A simple *I've had enough* followed by the sound of her feet striding briskly away.

Only a fool or a glutton for punishment would go after her.

Apparently, Reuben was just such a fool.

He raced to the door, then realized he was still shirtless. If Gladys didn't want him now, she'd appreciate him even less if he caused a half-naked scandal in the middle of the Blushing Maid Inn.

Cursing beneath his breath, he dashed back to the sofa and dove for his discarded garments. Never before had it taken so long to shove his fists into sleeves and fasten a half dozen buttons.

By the time he burst out of his room and into the public corridor, there was no sign of her. He ran to the stairs, first peering down, then up. Faint footfalls echoed overhead. Given it was a popular hotel in the middle of a packed festival, those feet could belong to anyone.

Reuben prayed their owner was Gladys.

He took the stairs two at a time, three at a time, skidding onto the waxed wooden landing of the floor above just as she was fitting a key into a door.

The beleaguered sigh she did not bother to hide as she turned to face him almost broke him.

Her eyes were flat and uninterested. "Did I leave something behind?"

"Yes." His voice scratched. "*Me.*"

She turned back to her door. "I meant to."

"There's not someone else, is there?" he blurted out, as fear and panic overtook him. "You said there wasn't."

She visibly gritted her teeth, then turned back

to him. "What I said was, I'm not a courtesan any-more. You can't buy me. I'm not for purchase."

He stared at her, uncomprehending. If she wasn't for sale, how was he supposed to win her? His looks, his body, and his bank account were all that he had to offer. If she'd already had her fill of the first two, and wasn't interested in the latter...

"I just thought—" he began.

"You've never thought," she said bitterly, the key shaking in her hand. "You haven't thought about me, or any of the unfortunates you use up and dis-card like disposable handkerchiefs. You think you're the flame of passion, but your fire is swift and destructive. There's not a line of happy smiles behind you, but a trail of ashes. I shall not allow you to burn me. Not again."

He frowned in confusion. "I would never do anything to hurt you."

"Never?" Her laugh was a broken looking-glass, humorless and sharp. "You are the cause of every-thing that has ever hurt me."

"What are you talking about? I just met you, in that statue garden—"

"*Yes*. In that statue garden. Five years ago, when I was a wide-eyed virgin who had never so much as been asked to waltz. You plucked me out of the darkness, just as you did this week, grabbing me to you without consent or concern, as if I were a dan-delion in your path, there to be admired for a mo-ment and then blown to smithereens."

"You..." he stammered, the blood draining from his face. Gladys was... Lady Dawn? The woman he'd been pining after for five long years? And she *hadn't* married Alsop? "Y-you..."

"Me," she confirmed, her eyes flashing. "Because of that kiss, I was instantly and irrevocably ruined.

I lost my reputation in the blink of an eye. My family was forced to disown me in order to save themselves. My suitor married my sister. And I became *this*." She gestured at her body. "A bauble, for men like you to play with, when they have too much time or money on their hands."

Horror drove waves of clammy gooseflesh along his skin. The blackguard who had destroyed her life... The blackguard Reuben himself had sworn to rend limb from limb... Was *him*.

He was the monster. The villain. The self-centered good-for-nothing that poisoned with his very touch and yet blithely continued doing so, without a care in the world.

"I do not need you," she enunciated, pronouncing each syllable with devastating exactness. "And I certainly don't want you." With a curl of her lip, she added, "*Or* your money."

"I didn't know," he managed to choke out. "I thought... I thought you had married Alsop."

"If that's true, it's because you didn't bother to listen to me when I told you my name. Just like you didn't listen to me today, when I told you I'm not for sale. No, I'm not my sister. Kitty's the one who got to keep her reputation, her standing in society, and my parents' love. I'm the one who lost everything, because I had the misfortune to come in contact with *you*."

"I thought... That night, I thought you were someone else. That's why I grabbed you. I was waiting for someone..."

"You discovered your mistake straightaway. If not from the first moment, then certainly when I looked you in the eye and told you my name was *Miss Gladys Bell*, and not whomever you'd expected. And then what? Nothing. You let the chips fall where they may. You flounced along to pollinate your next flower, as you always do, and I was sent penniless into the streets to pay for your mistake."

No, no, no. He staggered backwards. This was not what was supposed to happen. Then or now. He'd thought it was an innocent stolen kiss. Meaningless. Harmless. Instead, Reuben had inflicted more harm than he could ever imagine.

Reuben put his hands over his face. He wasn't innocent at all. He was guilty of every single thing she'd accused him of. He'd walked away. Actively chose to push her from his mind. Avoided all news of her.

Hadn't even bothered to check if he had the right name.

No wonder she'd fled from his embrace. He wasn't a catch. He was a nightmare. Insisting she play the role of whore—*his* whore—when she'd told him point blank that her sole desire was to make her own decisions, to choose her own partners. To live her life as *she* wished for once, rather than cater to the whims of spoilt and selfish "gentlemen" like him.

Reuben wasn't just not good enough for someone like Gladys.

He was poison.

CHAPTER 20

Gladys fled into her hotel room, shut the door tight, and flung her shoulders against it as though to keep out a charging bull. Or to keep herself upright.

She had done the thing she'd set out to do: snatch the toy out of The Despicable Medford's hands and break his heart.

It didn't feel nearly as pleasant as expected.

She'd also done what she'd sworn not to do: told him exactly who she was and how deeply he'd hurt her. Fat lot of good that had done. He'd looked startled, yes, but he hadn't even bothered to claim he was sorry.

Perhaps he wasn't sorry. Perhaps the only thing that had surprised him was that a woman had any thoughts and dreams or life at all outside of wishing to spend a moment in his storied arms.

Then good riddance of bad rubbish! She'd been a fool to want him, for a minute or a lifetime, then or now. It was time she wised up and used her eyes. Tigers didn't change their stripes, and rakes didn't gad about proposing marriage.

No one would propose marriage to someone like Gladys.

Originally true because she was a hopeless wallflower, and now even doubly true because of the opposite. She was too ruined to be wanted for anything other than a monetary transaction. The idea that she could be more than a temporary pastime didn't even cross men's minds.

Heat pricked her eyes and she blinked hard to rid herself of the brief weakness. She hadn't cried over Reuben's disinterest in years, and wasn't going to start back up again now.

She hated herself for believing, even for a moment, that he'd finally seen her for the entire person she was. That he chose her and valued her. That he could change. That an inveterate self-indulgent scoundrel like Reuben Medford actually wished to be her husband and a true partner. That his shriveled black heart knew what it meant to love.

"Imbecile," she muttered. "Rotten feathers for brains."

She pushed away from the door and hurried into her bedchamber, where she set about packing her valise as quickly as possible. She'd originally intended to return home in the morning, after the festival had ended, but she couldn't stand a single moment longer beneath the same roof as Reuben Medford.

With every fiber of her being, she longed to be back in the safety of her home, in her favorite chair, Count Whiskers on her lap, petting his soft gray fur and listening to the soothing sound of his low purr vibrating beneath her fingertips.

She closed her valise and dragged it to the

doorway, then rang the bell for aid. It was unlikely that Reuben was still out in the corridor—Lord knew, he hadn't bothered to knock with an apology—but there was no sense exposing herself to him anew without a burly footman or two as reinforcements.

When the knock finally did come, it was from the hotel's employees, as expected. It took them no time at all to bundle Gladys and her valise into a hackney carriage and send her off on her way back to London while it was still light.

The novel Reuben had scoured the earth for her taunted her from the seat cushion beside her. She wanted to set fire to it and anything else that reminded her of his face or his touch or the way she'd felt when she'd still hoped he actually cared for her. But burning a book was a step too far, even for a woman scorned as badly as Gladys. Especially a book as good as this one. It wasn't the intrepid heroine's fault she had been purchased by an arrogant, thoughtless cad.

Not that Gladys had proved herself particularly brilliant with this hare-brained stratagem. Oh, it had worked. After five interminable years, she'd got her revenge at last. But the cost was too great. She'd let him break her heart all over again.

The first time, she'd been naive. An innocent. A goose. But this time, she'd walked right into the same old trap with her jaded eyes wide open and her heart on a platter for him to eat up and spit out anew. She scooped up her pelisse and parasol and walked away from Reuben Medford and temptation.

Never again.

～

BY THE TIME she arrived in rainy London just after midnight, Gladys felt worse, not better. The dreary weather matched her spirits. She paid the driver extra to carry her valise to her door, then retrieved Count Whiskers from the neighbor and cradled her beloved cat to her chest, her cheek nestled against the top of his soft head.

"I won't leave you again," she whispered. "You're all the man I need."

He responded with a purr, and wrapped his tail around her head.

She carried him into the parlor and lowered herself carefully onto their favorite chair. They'd spent uncountable hours right here, her reading, the cat sprawled in her lap, sleeping or grooming himself or blinking sleepily as if completely flummoxed as to why on earth he was awake.

"That's how I feel, too," she informed him softly. "I want to sleep for forty hours straight."

But every time she closed her eyes, all she could see was Reuben. Grabbing her in the garden. Treating her like a trollop. Skipping rocks into the river. Offering to make her his mistress. Reading his godawful tomes stuffed with dry historical facts as though the contents were works of Byron. Eyes alight with mischief as he presented her with a picnic consisting purely of shameless aphrodisiacs. Toasting her ale with his own in the brewer's field. Surprising her with pudding. Losing good-naturedly at Casino. Eyelashes fluttering as he brought them both to climax.

Offering any sum she wished, if only she would exchange it for sex—and nothing more.

To her cynical surprise, there were far more good times than bad. They could have been good together. *If only.*

She buried her face in her kitten's soft fur and grieved for what might have been.

CHAPTER 21

*W*hen dawn came, Reuben hadn't slept a wink. He'd made the trip back and forth between his room and Gladys's a hundred times over the course of the night, and never quite managed to knock.

For one, he didn't wish to disturb her sleep—or her peace and quiet, if she was awake. He'd been significantly more than a mere "bother" already. He'd ruined her life. Destroyed her future. And his response to his impulsive actions was disgruntlement that a stranger whose name he hadn't bothered to learn had chosen Alsop over him.

Good God, the hubris.

It was a miracle Gladys had deigned to speak to Reuben at all. And no wonder he couldn't think of anything to say to excuse his inexcusable behavior. She'd had five long years to stew over the wreckage he'd made of her life, whereas he'd only just learned the extent of the harm done.

But the point wasn't to blame her for not informing him earlier. The point was that it shouldn't have happened, and once it did, he should've *known*.

176

What would it have cost him to pay a modicum of attention when she'd told him her name? Her relatives had yelled it out the garden door, for God's sake. There could be no claiming he'd missed hearing it.

Once he'd realized he grabbed the wrong woman, he should have done whatever was necessary to make it right. Which did not mean sending a debutante stumbling back into a ballroom with her bodice askew and her hair in disarray. He should've asked more questions of Alsop. What's more, Reuben should have found Gladys and spoken to her himself.

No—not words. She'd needed more than platitudes. Gladys had deserved immediate corrective action. He'd been the one playing with fire, whilst she was the one who had got burnt.

I've had enough, she'd said. An understatement. Reuben had managed to simultaneously do too much and not near enough.

The mystery wasn't why Gladys had walked away, but rather why she'd given him the time of day at all.

Time. The notion made him think of her hourglass. Of course she could only tolerate his presence in small doses. She should have sprouted the wings of an angel for refraining from slapping his face on first sight.

He couldn't leave Marrywell without giving her that opportunity. There was no apology on earth that would right the wrongs done to her, but he would stand there and take every blow if she wished to rail at him with her nails and fists.

As soon as the sun was at a semi-acceptable height, Reuben presented himself at her door and gave a firm knock.

She didn't answer.

He knocked a second time, and then a third. On the fourth knock, the door opened—revealing a sleepy-eyed older gentleman with an irritated scowl.

"What do *you* want?" the man barked.

"Er," said Reuben. "I'm looking for a Miss Gladys Bell…"

"Who?" The man gaped at him in bafflement. "You've got the wrong room. All you drunken bucks… When I was your age—"

The door slammed in Reuben's face, blocking out the rest of the man's tirade.

Gladys was gone. He'd taken too long. This time, the hopes his inaction had ruined were his own.

Though he knew it was useless, Reuben begged the proprietor of the inn, the keeper of the lending library, anyone he could think of, for clues as to where she'd gone. No one had an address for her. In fact, a "Miss Bell" had never registered at the inn. Nor was there a Gladys Smith.

With frustration, Reuben summoned his carriage and flung himself inside. Back to London, then. With luck, that was where Gladys had gone as well. Not that he was any more likely to find her in a crowded metropolis than he had been in a small country town.

He spent the hours of the long journey alternating between staring listlessly at the floor and burying his face in his hands. All the things he should have said flooded him now. *I'm sorry* was top of the list. Along with *I'll never forgive myself* and *I love you* and *Please give me a second chance.*

No—a *third* chance. She'd already given him a second one, and he'd bollocksed that up, too.

He'd been so afraid of her rejecting him, that he hadn't properly expressed that he accepted *her*. Not as a courtesan—which, as she pointed out, she'd explicitly told him she was no longer—but as a lover. As a friend. As a *person*.

He had offered to be her protector not because he was any good at protecting her, but because he'd been too scared to admit what he really wanted: Gladys. Forever. As his wife.

He'd known there would be no hope of her agreeing to that arrangement. He was nothing more than a trifling rakehell, whereas she...

Whereas she...

Had said, *I've never done this before, either.*

She wasn't talking about a financial relationship between mistress and protector. She didn't want such a thing, or expect him to offer it when she'd already made clear that she had moved on from those days. She'd wanted to pick her own partners, she'd said. To forge her own future.

Which meant, what she'd *thought* he'd been proposing was...

"Oh, God." Reuben dropped his face into his hands, his stomach flipping.

She'd thought he was proposing marriage. The thing he should have proposed five years ago when he'd left her reputation in ruins. The thing he should have proposed fifteen hours ago, when she was still naked and happy in his arms.

If it had been a hard sell then, it would be impossible to convince her now.

"You nodcock," he mumbled into his hands.

She didn't want his money. She wanted *him*. And she wanted him to want *her*.

Instead he had treated her like every other man had done before him. A path Reuben had put her on. A hell he'd had the opportunity to save her from forevermore. And failed to.

He hadn't just been the villain of the piece five years ago. He was the villain now, too.

"John Coachman!" He knocked on the driver's connecting panel just as the carriage was entering Mayfair. "I need you to take me to..."

Where? He didn't even know in which neighborhood Gladys might live. But *someone* had to. A courtesan operating in fashionable London for half a decade meant commensurately fashionable clients. *Someone* Reuben knew had to know where to find her.

"To my club," he ordered, leaning forward on his seat, his limbs vibrating with anticipation. "Make it quick!"

The carriage had barely slowed to turn down the right road, and already Reuben was leaping out onto the pavement, running past the street-sweeper and into the exclusive gentlemen's club with all the elegance of a runaway bull.

It took over an hour—and a round of rum on Reuben for half the patrons inside—but he soon had the information he needed.

"John," he shouted as he raced back to the carriage. Rather than waste time climbing inside, Reuben hoisted himself up next to his driver and handed him the address. "No time to waste!"

The truth was, Reuben might have nothing *but* time to waste. There was no reason to believe Gladys would open her door to him, much less listen to a word he said, or wish to spend another moment in his company.

The most likely scenario was that he was already too late. His chance to save the day had ended five years ago, and his opportunity to put things to rights had gone up in smoke last night.

But he had to try. Love was worth fighting for.

Gladys was worth any sacrifice.

WHEN REUBEN ARRIVED at her door, it was not empty-handed. He'd made a brief stop along the way, in the hopes that it would aid his cause. And if not... well. He would keep trying until there was no hope left.

He set the heavy basket on the doormat and banged the brass knocker.

Silence greeted him. And nerves. Pinpricks, all over his body. Nerves and desperation and—

A *miaow*. Soft, but right there on the other side of the door. Count Whiskers! Gladys had said a friend was minding her cat, which meant if Count Whiskers was now back at home, Gladys must be, too.

Reuben banged the knocker again with renewed hope.

"I'm coming," came her laughing voice as the lock disengaged. "What on earth can be the—"

She stared at him, her happy smile falling into an expression of dismay.

He dropped to his knees at once, clasping his hands in supplication.

Count Whiskers let out a hiss. Gladys moved to shut the door.

"Please listen, just for a moment," he blurted out, unable to tide the words now that he'd found her. "I'm sorry. I'm *so* sorry. I will never stop being sorry for what I did to you, and my lack of action that followed."

She crossed her arms, but she didn't shut the door.

"My chest isn't big enough to contain all the sorrow I feel. Made all the worse because my sorrow is meaningless. I'm sorrier than I can ever say, but that won't undo what I've done." His words spilled faster and faster. "I wronged you, time and again. I should have seen it then. I see it now. I see *you*, now."

She didn't move.

"And this is me." He spread his arms wide. "Worse than imperfect. You know the worst of me, because I showed it to you, again and again. I believed I caused no harm, when the opposite was true."

Her brow lifted slightly, as though to say, *Understatement.*

"I was a terrible person," he admitted. "I don't want to be the rogue anymore. I'd like to think I stopped being that man when I met you again for the second time—but we both know I kept hurting you. It probably doesn't help to know that my missteps this time were because I *did* want you, and was afraid you wouldn't want *me*."

Her eyebrows climbed higher. "The ton's most prolific rake somehow believed himself undesirable? I was literally naked in your arms."

The back of his neck heated. "And I thought that was all anyone ever wanted from me. On a hot summer day, cold sugary ice cream sounds delicious. And the first scoop *is*. Maybe even the second. By the third, you no longer hunger for it. By the fourth, your stomach starts to turn. By the fifth, you can't even bear to open your mouth. I'm not just an acquired taste. I'm only palatable in single scoops."

She crossed her arms. "You're a person, not ice cream."

"Yes, well, that's easy to say when you're clean spring water, perfect at any time of any day, and absolutely necessary for life. I could never get enough of you, Gladys. I would bathe myself in your embrace, drown in your kisses. I want you when you are boiling hot, and I want you when you pelt me with shards of hail. I want your puddles, your thunderstorms, your tsunami. I don't deserve any part of you, but would cross the farthest desert for a single drop."

"And here you are. On my doorstep."

"Tell me where you want me, and that is where I will go. On the moon? I will fly away. In your life? I will never leave it. I never truly wanted you to be my mistress. I want you to be my wife." He pulled a diamond ring from his pocket. It had belonged to his grandmother. "I know I don't deserve your presence before an altar yet. Take this, as a token of my sincerity. All I ask for today is a chance to prove it."

She did not take the ring. She scooped Count Whiskers up into her arms instead, and jutted her chin toward Reuben's knees. "What's in the basket?"

"The last resort of a desperate man." He flung open the lid. "Every book I could find with similar themes to the ones you've been reading. Including the next volume in that series."

She frowned. "The next installment doesn't publish for another month."

"And yet, publishers must print copies in advance, in order to be ready for release day." He held up the volume. It had cost a small fortune to pry it from the publisher's warehouse. "If you don't want it…"

Gladys shooed Count Whiskers into the house behind her and held out her palm. "Give it here."

Reuben obeyed, wishing she'd shown half as much interest in the diamond ring and the rest of his speech. Then he remembered he'd left out the most important part of all.

"I love you, Gladys," he said, speaking from the heart. "I've spent the past five years unable to think of any woman but Lady Dawn, and it was *you* I was searching for all along. I love you more than I believed it possible to love anything or anyone. Please allow me to spend the rest of my life proving the depths of that love. Whatever you need, I want to provide. Whatever you desire, I wish to give. Starting with every breath I take, and every beat of my heart, which pounds only for you."

Her eyes darted up from the book to meet his steady gaze.

"I mean it," he said softly. "Let me prove to you and to the entire world that Reuben Medford is the luckiest man who ever lived, because Gladys Bell blessed him with a smile."

The corner of her mouth lifted. "You remembered my name."

"I'll never forget it, or anything else about you. I am yours, and I want you to be mine. Whatever it takes. I realize that you cannot yet love me in return—"

"Oh, for Count Whiskers' sake, Reuben. Why would you still be here on my front step, if I didn't love you?"

His brain erupted into colorful fireworks. "You love me?"

"I'd have shut the door in your face, if I didn't

still harbor a foolish hope that you might say something I wanted to hear."

He held his breath, and proffered his grand-mother's ring. "And might you say in return, 'Yes, Reuben, I'll be your wife'?"

"Mm, close." She held up the contraband leather volume. "Perhaps more like, 'Thanks for the book; I'll be busy for the next five hours whilst I—'"

He scrambled to his feet and reached for her.

She threw her arms about his neck. "I'll consider your proposal on one condition."

He crushed her to him, terrified to let her go. "Anything you desire."

She tilted her head back to gaze up at him, eyes wide and twinkling. "Might I have a scoop of that ice cream now, please?"

"Now and all night long," he growled as he carried her into the house.

Neither of them ended up reading a word that evening after all.

EPILOGUE

Three months later

*M*rs. Gladys Medford lounged across her husband's broad chest on a picnic blanket beside a gently burbling stream, and closed her novel with a happy sigh.

"Thinking of our wedding again?" asked Reuben.

"Our what?" she teased, hugging the not-yet-released copy of the latest book in her favorite dramatic gothic adventure to her chest. "The castle is *haunted*. When the walls began to crumble down around the heroine, the long-dead spirits of the castle's previous victims rose from the rubble."

"Mm-hm," said Reuben. "It was a beautiful ceremony. Though I fear the addition of Count Whiskers might have been a bit much."

"He was not *much*!" she protested, whacking her husband's shoulder with the book. "He just wasn't quite clear on what to do with the ring, that's all."

"I wouldn't think 'cough it up in a hairball' was part of the plan."

"Well, I didn't hear you tell him *not* to. Next time, be more specific."

"There is no next time." He flung her finished novel onto the green grass, tossed her onto her back, and made growling noises as he nuzzled her face and neck. "There is only you and me, forever and ever. Say it."

"All right, I'll say it." She gave a long-suffering sigh. "It was bad ton of Count Whiskers to vomit up your grandmother's ring onto the parson's shoe."

"The wedding breakfast went better," Reuben agreed. "I was gratified to see you make up with your sister, though I'm glad you didn't invite your parents. They don't deserve you. Or our award-winning hospitality." He smiled in remembrance. "No one honked up wet furballs onto my award-winning pudding."

"I'm sure Count Whiskers would have done you the favor, if you'd asked nicely."

"Next time," Reuben promised.

Gladys bared her teeth at him and rubbed her nose against his. "There won't be a next time."

"We could make it a tradition," he offered. "Choose each other every year, on the same date."

"I choose you every morning and every night," she informed him. "I don't need the trappings of public displays to prove the value of my love."

"And yet, where is my grandmother's freshly polished ring now?"

She wiggled her fingers. "Here on my hand. Not going anywhere."

"What about us? Should we go back to Marry-well next year?"

"You already married well."

"Mm, but there's a shocking lack of statue gardens here in Battersea Park. How am I supposed to grab you against your will and ravish you senseless?"

"I'm very much a willing participant in every one of your wanton schemes, so you shall simply have to settle for ravishing me senseless."

He brightened. "At this very moment?"

"At the moment, we're in the middle of a public park."

"No one can see us."

"At least twelve other couples, twenty-five families, and a pair of gardeners can see us."

"Sure, but they're not watching. We're practically alone. What if I pull the picnic blanket atop us? Will that fool them then?"

"I have a better idea." She stretched out one arm to reach for her book.

"Don't tell me your better idea is to reread that story from the beginning."

"No, I'm tidying up. My better idea is getting out of here and finding a nice private place for a scoop of ice cream instead."

His eyes darkened with interest. "Ice cream, ice cream? Or... *ice cream?*"

She grinned at him wickedly. "Scooper's choice."

"I'll scoop *you* up," he rasped, and did just that. "I'm fairly certain I can make it to the back of our carriage before I rend your garments from your body and show you a better time than that crumbling old castle."

"I'm not sure *I* can wait that long." She wiggled her brows and held on tight. "Run fast."

And so he did.

As for the soft sounds that shortly emanated from the back of the carriage... well. John Coachman simply grinned to himself as he drove the long way home.

Again.

~

THANK YOU

AND SNEAK PEEKS

THANK YOU FOR READING

Love talking books with fellow readers?

Join the *Historical Romance Book Club* for prizes, books, and live chats with your favorite romance authors:

Facebook.com/groups/HistRomBookClub

Check out the **Patreon** for bonus content, sneak peeks, advance review copies and more:

https://www.patreon.com/EricaRidleyFans

And don't miss the **official website**:

www.EricaRidley.com/books

ABOUT THE AUTHOR

Erica Ridley is a *New York Times* and *USA Today* best-selling author of witty, feel-good historical romance novels, including THE DUKE HEIST, featuring the Wild Wynchesters. Why seduce a duke the normal way, when you can accidentally kidnap one in an elaborately planned heist?

In the *12 Dukes of Christmas* series, enjoy witty, heartwarming Regency romps nestled in a picturesque snow-covered village. After all, nothing heats up a winter night quite like finding oneself in the arms of a duke!

Two popular series, the *Dukes of War* and *Rogues to Riches*, feature roguish peers and dashing war heroes who find love amongst the splendor and madness of Regency England.

When not reading or writing romances, Erica can be found eating couscous in Morocco, ziplining through rainforests in Central America, or getting hopelessly lost in the middle of Budapest.

~

Let's be friends! Find Erica on:
www.EricaRidley.com